Because of Austin

J.J. Francesco

Book and cover design by Jansina
Front cover models: Braiden and Bekam Frady
Photographer and cover design consultant: Katy Neill
Back cover photo by Scott Webb on Unsplash
The text is set in "Libre Baskerville."
The display type is "I Love Derwin" (Robert), "Susie's Hand" (Conner), and "Unicorg Hand" (Austin, title, and all other instances).

ISBN: 978-1-63522-541-9

Printed in the United States of America
10 9 8 7 6 5 4 3 2 1

Rivershore Books
8982 Van Buren St. NE • Minneapolis, MN 55434
763-670-8677 • info@rivershorebooks.com

For Jamie and Noel

"There is no footprint too small
to leave an imprint on this world."

–Unknown

A Note for Parents and Teachers

I wrote *Because of Austin* with the intention of marketing it as an adult novel narrated by a child, a bit like Emma Donoghue's *Room*. Over time, advice from those assisting me with the project prompted me to consider also aiming it toward a younger audience. The book's coming-of-age themes about the importance and beauty of life, familial relationships, and how we treat other people seemed to make for a good educational read.

With that said, this book does deal with some dark and disturbing topics, including death, suicide, depression, light profanity, and some brief depictions of lethal injuries. The book may be too disturbing for certain readers. I do hope this book can serve as a powerful reminder to see the intrinsic value of human life, but I caution parents and teachers to exercise discretion when considering sharing it with a younger reader.

Included at the end of the book is a discussion guide with questions and suggested activities for parents and teachers to use to help younger readers comprehend and apply some of the themes of this story. Should readers decide embark on this journey with younger readers, my hope is that it can be a meaningful experience to strengthen relationships.

Chapter 1
Austin

He's trying to get me.

I back up against the bars on the jungle gym. The sun's hot so they burn, but I don't have anywhere else to go.

"What's wrong, Austin? Run out of places to run?" Robert takes another step closer. Then his shadow blocks out the sun.

"You win," I say. "Please, just leave me alone."

He laughs. "You're the one who invited me to your birthday, loser."

"I had to invite everybody in the class." I look down. Today's supposed to be my day. I'm turning 7 at 2:56 P.M. I want to play games with Conner and run in the elephant sprinklers. The playground has them on full blast today. They must've known it was my birthday.

Robert grabs the band of my bathing suit. "It's your birthday, so you have to wear your birthday suit." He laughs. "Come on, Birthday Boy. Stop fighting."

I wiggle out of his grip and lean over the edge. I see Mommy running around trying to make sure there's food all over my Pokémon birthday plates. My teacher, Ms. Wells, is helping her. I don't think they see Robert about to pants me. He did it at school twice this week and everyone laughed. He's so much stronger than me, so I can never do anything to stop him no matter how hard I try.

I look for Conner. He can keep me safe. Where is he? "Conner!" I shout to the playground.

Nobody hears me. Not even the kids from school I invited to my birthday party. I don't know if I'm their friend or not. We play at recess, but then they laugh every time Robert pulls my pants down or pushes me on the floor.

Robert yanks me back and sits on my chest. "You think you're leaving?"

"They're gonna throw you out without any cake or ice cream." I shut my eyes and scramble but can't get away. "Let me go. Let me go."

He drools on my face. "Why are you covered in drool? Are you a baby?"

"Stop it." I throw my fists at him, but I can't punch.

Then I feel someone throw Robert off me.

I roll into a sit and wipe my eyes on my arm.

Conner's standing over Robert. "Why are you even here? Nobody wants you, Robert. Go home."

Robert jumps to his feet. "Austin invited me."

Conner shoves Robert toward the slide. "Yeah, I know. He had to invite everybody he doesn't like in class. It's the rules. Nobody wants a dummy like you here. You wouldn't even be in his class if you were smart enough to go to the next grade."

Robert bites his lip and twitches. "Hey, I brought him a present."

"Yeah, take it back." Conner pulls me close to him. His skin is wet from the sprinklers. "If it's from you, he doesn't want it. Now go away."

Robert backs away and slides down the slide. He looks up from the ground. "You can't hide behind your brother forever, Austin."

I break free from Conner and stomp away.

"Why do you let him mess with you like that?" he says. "You can hit hard."

I jump onto the monkey bars and swing. "He's bigger and stronger and he's really mean." I pounce onto the ground.

Conner slides down the twirly slide and lands on his feet. "He only picks on you because you don't fight back."

"He pulls my pants down at gym class. I can't fight back and hide at the same time."

Conner chuckles and runs to the swing. He stands on it and starts swinging. "So what? I say, if he does it again, pee on him. That's what I'd do."

"But there are girls there."

Conner laughs. "I know. That's why it would be really funny."

I sit down on the swing next to Conner and start swinging. "I don't want to fight back. I want him to just leave me alone."

Conner jumps off the swing. "He ain't gonna. He's

Francesco

a jerk like that. But you can't keep letting him ruin your fun." He pushes me on the swing, like he used to when we were really little.

I move my legs back and forth and pretend like I'm flying in the wind.

"You're 7 now. You're a big boy." He stops my swing and motions at Robert. "You can't let creeps like him pick on you." Then Conner says that Robert is something we use to go to the bathroom.

"Don't say that word! Mommy will ground you."

Conner sticks his tongue out. "I'm 10 now. I can say whatever I want." He yanks me off the swing. "Now come to the sprinklers. It's freaking hot." He claps my back. "Hurry up."

He chases me into the sprinklers. The water's cold again because I got out for a long time. But it feels warm after a minute. I look down, so the water doesn't get in my nose. But then Conner takes a super soaker and squirts it at my belly. I laugh and look for one to fight back with, but all the other kids have them.

I see Robert lurking by a tree. He's staring at me with his "hate Austin eyes." I can tell that he wishes he was alone with me so he could beat me up. But Conner's here, so he won't let him.

Conner sees Robert too. He fills the soaker at the elephant sprinkler and pumps it at Robert's face with a laugh.

Robert yelps and covers his face and runs to his towel on the fence to dry himself. He says lots of bad

4

words into his towel, but I think I'm the only one who hears them.

"That's for pantsing my brother. Do it again and I'll aim lower."

Robert sits down at the table and doesn't look at me.

Conner puts his arm around me. "See? Fight back. It works."

"I guess." I look down. I don't want to tell him that I still wish that Robert could be my friend. And maybe one day he won't want to hurt me anymore.

Mommy calls us to have lunch, and then we have cake.

Everyone runs to sit down. I grab my Charizard towel and hang it over my shoulders.

Mommy lights 7 stick candles and a "7" candle with fake sprinkles on it. I feel the heat coming from the tiny flames as I lean over the cake. The dark chocolate icing looks cool.

Then everyone sings "Happy Birthday" to me. Conner claps and changes the melody to be funny.

I look over at Robert. He's looking to the side and moving his lips slightly, but I can tell he's not saying the words. He doesn't want my birthday to be happy.

"Make a wish and blow out your candles, Austin."

I inhale a huge breath and think about what I'd want to wish for. That Robert would be my friend. That I could see Daddy again. That Conner and I can play together forever. At least one of those might come true, as long as I don't tell any of them.

I blow out with all my might, and the candles all go out at once. The smoke smell goes up my nose.

Everyone claps, and Mommy pats me on the back and kisses my cheek. I smile and kiss her back.

She helps me cut the cake, a piece for everybody. Even for Robert, even though he doesn't deserve one. He eats it without looking at me. At least he didn't smash my cake.

I wave to the last kid to leave. He grabs his favor bag and runs to his dad's car without even saying goodbye or thanks. I keep waving anyway as they drive off. At least he doesn't make fun of me.

I see the bus coming and wave to the bus driver. He never waves back because he's usually in a bad mood, but he's never late. You can always count on Mr. Bus Driver.

"Austin!" I turn to Conner. He carries a bunch of my presents to the trunk of the car. "This is your stuff. Help me."

I run to him and grab a box just before it falls. "You almost broke my new chopper."

Conner rolls his eyes and tosses my stuff into the trunk. "Then you should put it all away, so if it breaks, it's your fault."

"You're just mad 'cause you ain't strong enough to carry it all." I stick my tongue out at him.

"That's it." He grabs me and squeezes me tight. He

picks me up a little, but he's not strong enough to lift me like Daddy used to.

I laugh and pretend to be scared. It's not scary when Conner does it.

"All right, boys." Mommy yanks me from Conner and sets me on my feet again. "No fighting. We have to finish cleaning up so we can get home. Just because you had off today doesn't mean you don't have school tomorrow. So no staying up late."

"Rats." I fold my arms and stomp to the picnic tables and gather all the used plates and napkins and cups into a trash bag. One of them still has a little soda left in it.

"Don't even think of drinking that, Austin." Ms. Wells folds the birthday tablecloth. "It's got somebody else's germs."

I dump it on the ground. "I wasn't gonna." Then I toss it in the bag.

Ms. Wells ties it up and tosses it in the trashcan. "Austin, I want to talk to you about something."

"I did all my homework."

She laughs. "No, it's not that. It's about Robert."

I look away and try not to let her see me look scared. "I don't want to talk about him." I start to walk away but feel her touch my shoulder to stop.

"I know he's picking on you."

"You never stop him."

She sighs and turns me to look at her. "I've talked with his dad a lot, and I've talked to him. But

I can't follow you two everywhere, and it seems like punishing him is only making him angrier."

"Conner wants me to fight back."

She flicks one of my tears away that I didn't even feel on my cheek. "No, fighting never solves anything. But you shouldn't just take it, either. You can stand up to him without fighting, and if that doesn't work, I might have to take more serious action."

"You mean kick him out?"

"Let's just try to work this out between the two of you, okay?" She pats me on the back. "Maybe tomorrow, we can all talk together at school?"

I don't want to talk about it at school. I just want Robert to be my friend or leave me alone. I don't like looking at him when he hates me. Having a teacher yell at him for being mean will only make him hate me even more. I can feel it when people don't like me. They make the air around them feel heavy, and then it feels like there are sharp razors crawling up my arms and legs until I walk away. Just thinking about her talking to Robert makes the razors show up.

I twitch and go to the car. "Okay," I say. But I hope she forgets.

Mommy hugs Ms. Wells goodbye and thanks her for helping with my birthday. Then she loads me into my booster seat in the back and Conner helps buckle me in. Robert calls me Carseat Boy every time he sees me. I hate being called that. But Mommy won't let me or Conner ride up front because we might fly through the windshield if a guy who can't drive hits our car like he did Daddy's.

As Mommy turns the corner for home, I see Daddy's old shop pass by. "Mommy, do you think Daddy knows it's my birthday?"

She doesn't talk for a moment, but I see her squeezing her lips. She never likes to talk about Daddy. She doesn't even like looking at me if she's thinking of him.

Conner grabs my hand. "Of course he does. Dad always remembered everything. He's probably trying to convince Saint Peter to let him send you a puppy."

"I want a parrot."

"Why do you want a parrot? They're so lame."

"They are not. They can talk. I'd teach him to call Robert a Peepeeface."

"All right you two." Mommy sounds not sad anymore. "We're almost home. Conner, I want you to help show your brother how to shower tonight."

Conner groans and rolls his eyes. "Do I have to?"

"Yes. I don't want to risk him falling and hurting himself. And you don't want to have to help him take baths forever. He's 7 now." She stops and breathes heavily. "I'd help, but I have to do some work for my boss . . ." She shoots a look to me as we turn down our street. "Did you have a good birthday, Austin?"

"Yep . . ." I rest against the soft seat and stare at the houses until we get to ours. Ours is the smallest on the street, but there's still lots of room for Conner and me to have our toys. It's a good house, but Mommy always says she has to do more work so we can keep it. I miss her when she has to work a lot and she can't play with me and Conner, but at least we don't live on the street and have to beg people to give us sandwiches so we don't starve. And Conner makes sure I don't get lonely. I know I'm annoying, but he never wants to play with any friends anyway, so we're all we got. But we're enough. If Robert didn't hate me, everything would be almost perfect, even if I wish Mommy was home more.

Chapter 2
Conner

I duck under Austin's birthday streamers to get into our room. I spent half the night trying to put them up while he was asleep so they'd be there as soon as he opened his eyes. Then he spent half the day going on about it, thanking me. I pretend like I don't like him acting all annoying but I'm glad he likes it. I wish he hadn't broken my camera last year or else I'd take lots of pictures so we'd remember where every streamer was.

The beat of his running footsteps echoes down the hall. "Conner! Mommy says we can take a bath instead tonight because it's my birthday and we can shower next year." He darts past me and jumps on the bottom bunk of our bed and hugs his stuffed dinosaur puppet that he loves for some reason.

"Austin . . ." Mom's voice, really meaning "Austin, stop lying to your brother" without saying it.

He knows it and pouts. "I don't like showers." He folds his arms and kicks his feet into the air and tries to pretend like he's riding a bike. Only his circles are more like lines.

"You haven't even taken a shower before."

"Because I don't like them. I like baths because there's bubbles and we can play."

"Whatever . . . let's just get this over with." I think Mom is just trying to save on the water bill again. Austin's a wimp but he can take his own shower without killing himself. It's not like it's hard. You use soap and shampoo and wash it off. But I can't tell Mom that. She's Mom and that means we just do it.

Austin's already undressed. He leaves his bathing suit in a heap on the floor.

"Austin, Mom will freak if she sees that on the rug. It's still not dry." I swipe it up and bring it to the bathroom towel rack to dry.

Mom strolls in and Austin quickly ducks behind the shower curtain. "You're a girl. No girls can come in when we're in here."

Mom chuckles and ruffles his hair. "I gave birth to you both, you know. Do what your brother says and be careful. No horsing around, you two. And remember, lights out by eight-thirty, which includes story time, so don't take too long." She looks to her room. "I have some work to do, but you know where to find me if you need me."

"Right . . ." I wave her out and shut the door. I sigh and lock it so she doesn't come in. She tells me not to lock the door but she won't know.

Austin sits in the tub part of the shower with his sad face. Not gonna work.

I step in with him and yank him to his feet. "I ain't

gonna keep doing this with you, so you gotta learn how to take care of yourself. Look, it's just like a bath only you stand." I move his hand to the shower nozzle and we pull it.

The shower blasts cold water in Austin's face. He cries and jumps back. "That's too cold."

I move his hand to turn it to the left. The water gets warmer. "Better?"

He jumps on my back and wraps his arms around my neck.

"I got you. Now you do what I say."

He leans his bony arms into mine and laughs. I let him have just a minute to think he's stronger than me because it's his birthday. Then I flip him off, piece of cake.

He lands on his feet but begins to slip and scream.

I grab him and steady him. "Be careful. This is why Mom makes me watch you." Maybe I shouldn't have said that.

"You saved my life. I could've cracked my head open like an egg and then my brains would be going all down the drain and Mommy would ground you."

I roll my eyes. Crazy like usual.

I grab his Banana Minions shampoo and dump a blob on his hair. "Just like a bath, you suds it." Then I take mine, blueberry and no stupid minions on it for little kids. We suds our hair until we both look like our hairs are made of bubbles.

"Why is your hair so much lighter than mine?"

Questions again. Austin thinks I know everything. I'm much smarter than him but I still don't know everything. Last time he asked about down there and I didn't know and he laughed at me. I don't care what Mom says. If he asks that again, I'm out of here and he can bang his head all he wants. Maybe it'll make him less annoying.

"My hair isn't that light." I rinse my hair and make sure he gets all the shampoo out of his. The water at our feet becomes slippery. "My hair is just light brown like Mom's is. Yours is dark brown like Dad's. It's got something to do with genes or something."

"But Mommy's hair is yellow."

"Yeah, because she makes it yellow."

I go to grab the bar of soap. Then I slip.

Then Austin grabs me. "Now I saved you. See? You shouldn't do it alone either. We should take baths again."

I throw the dove bar at him. "Nice try. What's the big deal anyway?"

"I like playing with you because nobody else will play with me and I know you will always keep me safe."

I help him soap his body down with the soap bar. I take our scrub sponge and help him scrub his back. I notice a bruise on it. "Hey, you didn't have this earlier." I touch it and he twitches. "Did he do this again?"

Austin's still. I turn him around and see his eyes teary.

"I told you, you have to fight back. You can't just let him pick on you and I can't always follow you around to kick his butt."

"But I'm scared. He's bigger than me. He's almost your age. Why is he in my class?"

"Because he's stupid."

"I can't fight him back. He'll kill me. I just want him to leave me alone. I don't like everyone laughing at me."

Nobody should be laughing at my kid brother except for me. I feel like I should go to school and beat them all up, but that'd only get me kicked out and he'd be alone again. "You're not weak. You just think you are. Fight him back. If he tries to pull your pants down, pull down his first. If he hits you, hit back harder. Kick him in the balls. You know it hurts when you get kicked there, so do that."

"Yeah, I kicked you there once." He giggles.

"You try it again and I'll kick yours harder."

He throws suds at my face.

I try not to let him catch me smile. "See? Just stop being afraid and just fight back and he'll stop picking on you because that's what bullies like him do. They run scared."

"Why does God let me get bullied? Am I bad?"

"Austin, I don't know. Stop asking so many questions."

He turns his head down and looks so sad and sulky. "Okay, I'll never ask you another question ever again."

He tucks his arms behind his back.

Is he trying to make me feel bad, or is he really upset? It's hard to tell with Austin. He sounds sad, but he's also a little goof so maybe it's all part of his master plan to make me feel bad.

"Yeah, right . . ." I say, hoping we can move on.

He pouts and turns away. "I miss Daddy."

I don't know what to say to him. I miss Dad too. I don't know if Austin even remembers him sometimes, but then he says something like this and I live it again.

Austin takes the sponge and scrubs down my back. "Come on, we gotta get done so Mommy doesn't yell and come in."

I laugh. "You're so weird . . ." I finish cleaning down and wash off and then shut the water off. I grab Austin's towel and wrap it around him and then do the same with mine.

We go to our bedroom and Austin slips into his Pikachu pajama top and his tighty whities. It's so hot out and Mom didn't turn the air on yet, so we don't wear bottoms. I put on my Iron Man shirt. He's cooler than Pikachu.

Austin throws his arms around me and hugs me. "I love you, Conner."

Weird. Why is he doing this now? I start to ask but then he'll never stop talking. I hug him and say "I love you" back.

I turn on our ceiling fan. It's crayons. I think it's silly, but Austin still likes it.

16

We brush our teeth and pee one more time. We wash our hands with the foam soap and go back to our room.

Austin gets on his knees and talks to Jesus and Mary. I do it too but let him do the talking. He thanks them for a good birthday and asks them to make it hurry up so it can be next year and he can wear the white suit and have Jesus. He goes to bless himself to close the prayer, but I get in a mention for Robert to get his butt kicked for teasing my brother.

I look at the clock and it's fifteen minutes until bedtime.

I walk into Mom's room. She's asleep at her desk, with papers with lots of long numbers under her arms.

I nudge her. "Mom, we're done. It's time to tuck us in."

She jolts awake and snaps to her feet. "I was just catching up on some work I missed. How'd the shower go?"

I shrug. "Austin didn't split his head open and his hair smells like bananas. It's his birthday so he gets his song and a story."

She laughs and hugs me, then follows us into our room. Austin's already in bed hugging the dinosaur puppet.

I climb up to the top bunk and pull back the covers.

Mom sits on the side of Austin's bed. "Did you have a great birthday?" She asked him that earlier. Doesn't she believe him?

Francesco

Austin smiles and kisses her. "I loved it. You made a great party."

"Tomorrow you can look at all the toys you got once you finish your homework."

"Can I take a shower with Conner again? It's not so bad and it's fun like a bath because the water hits Conner's face."

Mom laughs and starts singing him his lullaby song. It's some stupid thing she wrote when he was born that is mostly just his name made into silly rhymes. "Austin! Austin! Birthday man! His farts smell like a dog food can," I say. I smile and meet Mom's disapproving eyes. How dare I rap over her song! Austin laughs. At least he likes it. It was for him, anyway.

Mom then leads into Austin's nightly story that both of them pretend is not about this Austin but another one. In today's story, Austin turned 7 and had a birthday party at the playground and got to play in elephant sprinklers and eat chocolate cake and was a big boy and took his very first shower. She doesn't even try to make stuff up, but Austin just laughs and eats it up and then farts. Then he giggles for over a minute.

Mom scolds him with a laugh and then kisses him goodnight. "Happy Birthday," she says.

Then she reaches up to me and kisses me goodnight. "Thanks for helping him, Con. You know I appreciate how you take care of him."

I look away. "Goodnight, Mom."

I hear Austin get out of bed and look up.

He goes to the window and stares out at the moon.

"What are you doing, Austin? If Mom sees you out of bed, she'll spank you. We got school tomorrow."

"I can't sleep. I'm thinking about Daddy. I wish he was at my birthday."

My chest starts to hurt. "Yeah, well, he's with Jesus now."

"I know. I just miss him so much. And now Mommy has to work a really long time so we have enough money and so she ain't home much. And soon you'll be a big boy and you won't play with me or do anything with me anymore and I'll be all alone."

"I'm never going to be too big to play with you." I lean in close. "I might want to take my own shower, but that doesn't mean I won't play with you."

Austin turns to me. "Thank you, Conner." He crawls back into bed and I hear him snoozing in a few minutes.

Austin screams. Not a long one, just a single loud shout followed by fast panting. I peek down and see him sitting up, covered in sweat.

I jump down and wrap my arms around him. "It's okay, Austin. It was just a dream. Just a dream."

He cries and buries his head on my shoulder. His face is really wet. I lay him down again. "Try to go back to sleep."

He tugs my sleeve. "Stay. Please."

I kiss his forehead. Mom always says it looks like a moon. With only the moonlight coming in, I kind of see it. I also see his sad brown eyes staring at me so scared and thinking I'm the only one who can keep him safe.

"Okay." I hug him tighter until I hear him drift off again. I thought of asking him what the nightmare was about, but given how much he was shaking, it didn't matter. The only thing that matters is making sure he's safe.

Chapter 3
Austin

Conner pours me Shredded Wheat in a bowl. I like that it's sweet on one side but good-for-you on the other, so Mommy is happy and I am happy.

I loosen my school tie. It cuts my neck and makes me hot. I like our gym uniforms best. They are blue and not tight. But gym is on Tuesday, and today is Thursday.

Conner gulps a mouthful of cereal. He spills some milk on his tie. "Shoot." He wets a paper towel and rubs the tie until the milk is all gone. "We're gonna be late, darn it. Mom's gonna freak."

Mommy comes in and pours herself cold coffee. She drinks it with a sour face. "I am not going to freak, because we are all going to be on time today." She looks in a spoon and tries to straighten her hair. "I'm going to be staying late at the office. We have a budget meeting, so Ms. Wells was nice enough to let you stay with her until I get off. So you both be good for her."

"We will," I answer for both of us, as I chug another bite of cereal and sip my orange juice.

Conner rolls his eyes. "Didn't they just have one of those last week?"

Mom leans in and kisses him quick without hugging him. "Well Con, grown-ups talk about money things a lot, especially in companies. I need the overtime anyway. The bills aren't exactly getting lower."

"You can just get rid of one of us." He pushes his bowl away. "Maybe that'll save money. I can go live on a farm, or something." He bangs his chair out and stomps over to his backpack on the couch.

"Conner, I don't have time for this." Mommy holds her head and spills the cold coffee into the sink. "You know I love you and your brother, and we're not getting rid of anyone. All the stuff we use every day just costs money, and that means I have to work a lot of hours."

He swings the backpack over his shoulder. "Let's just go to school. Guess we're not going to go there next year, right? You'll send us to public school 'cause it's free." He walks to the door.

Mommy runs after him and stops him. "Hey. Don't talk like that to me. It's not easy, but I want you and Austin to get a good Catholic education. Yes, it'd be cheaper to send you to public school, but I love you both so I make the sacrifice. Luckily they work with us to make sure we can find ways to pay for it. But even if they didn't, I'd still send you because I care about you learning and want you to have the best education in the city." She turns Conner's head up. "I know it's hard sometimes, but I'm trying."

Conner shrugs. "Me too. Maybe you can just send

Austin next year. I already had my Communion. You can save money on me next year." He opens the front door.

"Conner, you didn't finish your breakfast," I say. "You're gonna be starving."

"I'm not hungry. I'll be outside. Hurry up. I don't want to be late for class again."

Mommy sinks into Conner's chair and lays her head down. I think I hear her crying a bit but can't tell because it's so silent.

My cereal's done so I put it in the sink with a little water. I walk over to Mommy and hug her. "Conner loves you, Mommy. We just miss you a lot. But you work hard to take care of us. Conner's just in a bad mood. He knows you're a good Mommy and I do too." I kiss her cheek.

She looks up and smiles at me. Her eyes are wet. She pulls me into a tight hug. "Austin, don't ever grow up, okay? You might become an old cynic like your mom."

"What's a clinic?"

"Cynic." She chuckles. "It's just somebody who thinks everything is sad and bad, even the good stuff."

"Like Conner?"

She shakes her head. "Conner's just being Conner."

"Do all grown-ups become like that? How do I not grow up?"

Mommy's quiet a moment. "No, I guess not. Some do find a way to keep that childlike innocence. I guess life just makes it hard to stay that way when you get older and see lots of bad things."

I smile. "Well then, I'll stay a kid forever just for you."

"I didn't mean what I said, not literally." She gulps. "I love you as my little boy, and you always will be no matter how big you get. But you and your brother have to grow up. You don't have a choice. Maybe just try to always remember how you think about things now, how you see the good things that Mommy doesn't see. And even after you are big and strong, you can still see the good things."

"Okay." I smile and hug her again and then run outside to Conner.

He leans against the car with his arms folded. "What's taking so long? Hustle."

"Is that your word for the week, Conner?" Mommy closes the door behind her as she walks out of the house, with my backpack in her hand. She swings the loop around my shoulder. "Almost forgot this, Austin. Don't want to show up to school without your books."

Conner shoves me as I climb into the car.

I laugh and shove him back. He may be stronger, but Mommy is here. So I always win.

School is all decorated for the First Holy Communions we're gonna have on Saturday. Everyone in second grade is going to wear white and go up to receive Jesus. It looks like a piece of real thin bread but is really still Jesus.

Mommy drops us off at the curb and waves goodbye.

Conner steps in front of me. "Wait for me right outside the door when we get out, okay?"

I walk past him when I see Father Doyle standing outside, as the second graders line up. They're still in uniform, but I saw some in their white outfits. I remember when Conner had his. He wore white everything. Suit, tie, even shoes. I remember when I laughed at him because the only thing that wasn't white was his underwear. All the girls wore pretty white dresses and things on their heads. Everyone looked so awesome and I couldn't breathe while seeing them. I knew soon it would be my turn, and I could wear white and receive Jesus too. Mom says we'll have to fit Conner's suit on me, since I'm a lot smaller, unless I grow big by next year. Then maybe it'll fit me.

Father Doyle sees us and waves. I run up to him. "Are you going to say Mass for them?"

He smiles and nods. "Well, we're going to just practice today."

"I can't wait until I am old enough to have Jesus."

He smiles and pats my head. "You're a real special boy, Austin. I wish most of the kids were as excited as you. Between you and me, I think many of them just do it because they think they have to."

"That's not right. They get to have Jesus. They should be so excited."

Francesco

He smiles. "You're going to be great in class next year, Austin. I hope you stay that excited. We can all stand to follow your lead. Now, why don't you two head to class? I don't want to make either of you late. I'll see you in Church, Sunday."

"Have fun in class, Austin." Conner runs ahead and leaves me alone in the hallway.

I see Robert pass by. He smiles at me. "Hope you had a fun birthday, Austin."

We walk into class together. Ms. Wells is sitting at her desk. She smiles when we come in.

He shares a glance with her. "Thanks for inviting me to your party."

Why is he being so nice to me? Does he finally want to be my friend? But then why do I still feel so scared standing next to him? It's weird. Even though he's smiling and seems nice, there's a certain look in his eyes. Like he still wants to hurt me and is just trying to put on a show for Ms. Wells. He's a whole huge six inches taller than me, so maybe he's just always scary because he's still in first grade with me and not third like he's supposed to be.

She walks up to the two of us. "Austin, I had a talk with Robert in the halls. I'd like it if the three of us could have a talk?"

I look down and pocket my hands. I don't want to talk. If Robert is thinking of being nice to me now, I don't want him to change his mind.

I hear the bell ring. Suddenly the entire class runs

in, like they were waiting in the hallway for every second away from the teacher.

I see Hillary not dressed in her school jumper but regular clothes. So does Ms. Wells. She has to go give her a demerit now, so I don't have to talk to her.

Before she goes, she taps us on the shoulder. "I still want to talk with you both after school. But in the meantime, I've switched your desks so you sit next to each other. I want you two to learn to get along, and if you start fighting, I'll see. You two could really be great friends if you just tried." She smiles and walks over to yell at Hillary.

I sit down and take out my books and put them in my desk. Robert sits at his desk and stares at me. His smile is gone, but he doesn't look mad yet. But I still feel scared.

Especially because he still keeps looking at me. What does he really want?

The morning was boring. We did Spelling and Math and Phonics. Only Religion was interesting because we talked about Jesus and Mary. After lunch, Ms. Wells says we can do an art project. She says we're supposed to draw our family and then cut it out so it's like 3D.

I get out my pencil and draw the lines for me first. I draw my favorite shirt on and my sneakers. I also draw a parrot on my shoulder, even though we don't have one yet. I draw Conner next to me with his baseball cap on. He doesn't wear it anymore, but he looks so cool in it. I draw Mommy with her work suit on and her briefcase that she keeps all her counting papers in. Then I draw Daddy in the clouds with Grandpa and Jesus and Mary and an angel. I don't give Daddy wings because Mommy and Father Doyle say people become saints and not angels. But I give him a yellow glow because everyone is bright and happy in heaven. Then I color in the rest of us. I use peach for our skin. It looks weird but is the only color that is close.

I take out my scissors. I lost the last pair after Halloween, and Mommy yelled at me and told me that we don't have the money to keep buying new ones. I didn't think they were that expensive, but Mommy told me it was the principal. I don't know what she has to do with my scissors, but I told her I'd take better care of these. They are bigger than my old ones because we just used an older pair we had in a drawer that wasn't too big for my fingers. They're sharper too, so I have to be careful not to cut myself, but I'm a big boy so I can use them.

I cut out the white around us. I am bad at making the round parts, so they are all pointy. But the white falls off, and our family 3D is done and looks really pretty. I can't wait to show Mommy.

Robert swipes the scissors from my hand and starts cutting out a drawing of him and his dad.

"Hey!"

Robert doesn't look at me. "You have to share. It's

in the Bible."

"Well, you could've just asked to borrow them."

"I'm not borrowing. They're mine now."

No they're not. Mommy's going to be so mad if I come home with them lost again. "Hey, you can't take them. Give them back. They're not yours."

He zips them in his pencil case and stuffs it in his backpack. "Are now."

"But I'll get in trouble."

"Sucks to be you, loser."

I look at his bag and wonder if I should try and take it, but Ms. Wells is watching and I don't want her to see us fighting. So I just sit here quietly. I try not to cry, but I feel a tear on my cheek. I wish Conner was here to take them back for me, but I'm too weak on my own. I don't know what I'm going to tell Mommy. Maybe she won't be mad if she knows it wasn't my fault.

I sit alone in class after the final bell rings and everyone else runs out, including Robert with my scissors. I know I'm supposed to meet Conner, but I don't want to move yet because then I might cry.

Ms. Wells sees me sitting as she puts all our tests in her teacher bag.

"Austin, you don't have to wait in here. You can go outside with Conner. I won't leave without you."

"I'm cleaning my desk."

She laughs. "Yes, I can see how clean it looks. You

can do that tomorrow, of course."

"I don't wanna go. I'm sad. Mommy will yell."

"What's wrong?"

"Robert stole my scissors." Why did I say that? I didn't want her to know, but it just came out.

"What? I thought you two were doing better." She takes a seat next to me. "I'm sorry. I shouldn't have tried to force you two to be friends. I just know kids like Robert, and they usually just want to be liked."

"I want to be his friend, but he's so mean . . . and now Mommy's going to yell like last time because she's going to have to buy new scissors, and we don't have the money."

She chuckles. "I don't think a dollar pair of scissors will make your mom broke, Austin."

I shrug. I don't know how much money we have.

She makes me stand up with her. "Tell you what. I'll help you get the scissors back, and then you won't need new ones. If you smile and get ready to leave. Deal?"

I smile and say "Deal." I high-five her.

We walk out together. Then she stops. "I just remembered. I had some more work in my desk I wanted to get done tonight. I'll be right back. Stay here." She disappears back into class.

I lean against the wall with last week's art projects of the carnival. I drew a roller coaster.

Then Robert comes over. I thought he went home.

"What do you want?" I take a step back. "Ms. Wells

is still here. She's taking me home."

Robert grins, but I can tell it's not real happiness. "You're a little tattle, aren't you? Can't fight me on your own and can't have your brother all the time, so you tell the teacher?"

"I just want you to stop teasing me."

"Teacher's pet, going home with the teacher. Does she keep you in a doggy bed too?"

My breathing gets heavy. Where is Ms. Wells? "She's just being nice."

He takes out my scissors and swings them on his finger. "These are yours, right?"

I nod. "Yes. They're mine. Give them back."

"Prove you're not a wimp and take them."

I reach for them, but he pulls them back. I jump.

He swipes them away.

"Give 'em. They're not yours. Go have your dad buy your own."

He lifts them higher. "Too short? Sucks to be you."

I remember what Conner told me about fighting back. I want to run away. I don't care about the scissors, but if I don't get them back, he'll never stop.

I pull my leg back and kick him right in the peanuts.

He groans and holds his crotch and says bad words to me.

I run to grab the scissors, but he pulls them away. "You'll never get them now."

I lean in to grab them. "You're not going to take my stuff anymore."

I see his hand swing forward.

Then the worst pain I ever felt shoots into my side, and then spins through my whole body. I want to scream. I want to cry. My mouth just hangs open and a puff escapes.

He steps back with my scissors in his hand. They're covered in all gooey red. My blood. Oh no. He stabbed me! He killed me!

I can't stand anymore. Everything is spinning. I grab my side and feel it sticky, and my hands get red on them.

I tumble to the floor. Then I feel so sleepy, and I can't keep my eyes open. I'm sorry, Conner. I should've been stronger. Then he couldn't have killed me like this.

Chapter 4
Robert

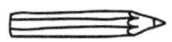

I didn't mean to stab him! I was just trying to keep the darn scissors away from the little wimp. I can't believe he kicked me in my nuts. Usually he just cries and runs to Conner. I wasn't even thinking about how sharp the scissors were. They're just for cutting paper. They aren't like a knife, but they still go into his side. Then blood starts coming out everywhere. On my hands and dripping onto the floor.

I pull out the scissors, and they are covered in blood. I drop them and take a step back as Austin looks at me with teary eyes. I've never seen anyone look so scared, and I almost want to help him. But if anyone sees me, I could get in trouble.

He hits the ground and his eyes close. Is he dead? Oh my God, did I kill him? I don't know how to check his neck to see if he's still alive.

I see our class door open and make a run around the side of the hall. I peek around when I hear Ms. Wells scream. She scoops him into her arms, and his legs and arms drag off the side. There's a huge red spot on the floor.

"Austin, can you hear me? What happened? Who

did this?"

Austin moans. He's still alive. But he doesn't say anything. Does she see the scissors? Does she see me? Am I going to jail?

She storms out of the doors with Austin, and I hear it slam shut. Then silence and painful quiet. I can hear my breaths and Austin's voice echoing in my mind.

I slide to the floor with my back against the wall. Then I squeeze my nuts, which I remember are still throbbing. I didn't think he could kick so hard, but this really hurts. But they must not hurt as much as getting stabbed. Those scissors aren't that big, but Austin is little too. What if he dies? I hate him, but I don't want him dead. Oh, please God, don't let him be dead.

I risk looking again. I see the blood spot and the bloody scissors. I think about taking the scissors so they don't find them as evidence. Maybe I can throw them out before anyone sees.

I take a step toward them, but then I hear someone coming. So I run the other way. I run out a back door, and then I run and run until I'm home.

No car in the driveway. Dad's not home yet.

I don't want to track blood into the house, so I run out back. I turn on the hose and wash Austin's blood off of me. I see the red water running down the patio.

I look at my uniform and notice a few flecks and smears of red. Darn, now I gotta get rid of this too if I can't get the red out. How am I going to explain it to

Dad?

I take off my shoes and strip to my underwear. I unlock the back door with the key from my backpack and go inside, keeping my clothes crumpled into a ball. I dash for the laundry room and throw my clothes in the sink and start washing. I don't know how to use the washer, so I just pour the detergent into the sink and wash and wash. But the red won't come out. It just won't come out.

I begin to cry. I don't want to go to jail.

Then I hear the front door open, and Dad announces he's home. He calls, "Robert. Robert, I brought a surprise home."

I don't respond, but I try to quiet a cry. He calls again.

I can't take it anymore. The blood won't come out. What can I do? "Dad!"

Chapter 5
Conner

Maybe it's the way Ms. Wells screams my name as she comes out the front doors.

It's like my entire insides run into each other. I feel like I have to pee and poop fire, and my stomach twists and spins. And then I turn around and I see him.

Austin, in her arms, leaking a trail of blood.

"Austin!" My throat stings from how loud I scream. "What happened?" I'm already crying, and then I see his side. "Is he dead?"

Ms. Wells runs to her car.

I get into the back next to Austin.

She has me press a blanket from the back seat hard against his wound and tells me to keep holding it tight for as long as I can.

"Aren't you calling 911? Who did this? What happened?"

She gets behind the wheel of her car, and the brakes squeak. She speeds onto the road and runs past the stop sign and a red light.

"What about the ambulance?"

"There's no time. I can get him to the hospital faster than they can get to us. Hold on tightly."

My hands are already sticky red, and the blood is coming through the blanket.

"Conner . . ." Austin moans but doesn't open his eyes.

"Don't try to talk. I'm here." My voice is choked, and my chest is hammering. I try to make him feel better, but his eyes spin a bit like in a scary movie and make my insides twist more. I've never seen him like this before. This is real blood, not movie blood. It's so much worse coming out of him.

"I didn't . . ." He coughs up a clop of blood in my face, and a small trail of blood runs down from his mouth.

I know from TV that this is bad. "Ms. Wells. He's bleeding out his mouth."

Austin's gasps come faster. I've never seen Ms. Wells so scared. I can see sweat rolling down her neck. When grown-ups are scared, it must mean it really is bad.

I hear the car scream louder and almost fall over, as Ms. Wells turns into the hospital parking lot. She stops in front of the emergency room doors.

Austin opens his eyes for just a second. I see tears and fear in those small brown eyes. Then he mumbles something I can't understand.

I lean in closer and squeeze his hand tighter. "What?" He slips away again. But I heard him. "Robert."

I follow Ms. Wells through the doors. Before I even get in and catch a breath, the doctors rush over with stretchers and a mask that gives Austin air.

Ms. Wells steps back, and her dress is covered in blood.

I look down and see my uniform is ruined with blood too. It looks even scarier on the white shirt.

I look at my hands and they are red too. Everyone is looking at us, and the doctors are asking all kinds of questions that Ms. Wells can't even keep up answering. I hear "scissors" and "floor" and a few other words.

As they wheel him off to operate, I shout out, "He's allergic to penicillin."

Everyone freezes a moment, like they don't know what to say. I don't even know why I said it. I just remember hearing it every time Mom took me and Austin to the kid doctor to get check-ups. They always asked Mom if we had any allergies, and that was one of Austin's. Mine was shrimp.

"Thank you for telling us," one of them says before they disappear behind swinging doors with Austin.

My stomach attacks me, and I fall into Ms. Wells' arms, crying as she cradles me close. What if I never see him again? My brain is still spinning, and this all feels like a really bad nightmare. I just want to wake up and see Austin sleeping below my bunk.

Please be a dream. Please be a dream.

"It'll be okay." She strokes my hair.

I clutch a fistful of her dress and try to tell myself

Austin isn't dead. I just don't believe it yet. Not with his blood all over us.

Austin's blood comes off my hands after five minutes of scrubbing in the sink. I stare as it washes red down the drain. That used to be in his body.

I try to wipe away the stains from my uniform with a wet paper towel, but I think that just makes it worse. Luckily, I have a change of shorts and a shirt in my backpack that I was supposed to wear at Ms. Wells' house. So I take off my uniform and throw on the extra clothes.

When I get out of the bathroom, we put my uniform in a plastic bag. Ms. Wells still has the blood on her dress.

I stare at it, never realizing Austin had so much of it in him. He's so little. "Don't worry about me," she says. "I can go home and change once your mom gets here."

"Did you talk to her?"

"I can't get a hold of her." She taps her cell phone. "I'm worried. She never turns her phone off."

"Sometimes she does if she's in a meeting and doesn't want her boss to fire her for not doing her job."

I clutch my backpack and Austin's. His is so light next to mine. They just left it on the floor when they took him back. It's been over an hour.

Doctors come out and ask questions. Like about Austin's name and that long number I can't ever remember the name for. They say they can look up his medical records so they know anything they need to.

Cops are here, and they talk to me for a minute. But mostly to Ms. Wells, since I didn't see anything.

They say they found the scissors at the school. The cops are all there now. Ms. Wells tells them that Robert stole them from Austin.

"Austin said his name in the car," I say. They all look at me and run to ask me more questions I don't know the answers to. It's like when Dad died. The cops only talked to Mom then, but I remember all their questions. I try to tune them out because seeing them makes it feel like Austin's dead.

Mom is crying when she runs through the doors. She rushes to the desk to ask where Austin is, but the desk lady won't let her finish talking. A man who looks like a cop, but isn't, tries to keep her back.

Mom sees us and runs over. She falls into Ms. Wells' arms. Then she screams and says things I can't understand.

"I just turned my phone off for one hour. I didn't want to, but he said no interruptions," she says. She cries harder and asks where Austin is. She asks what happened. She looks at me and hugs me. Then says I was supposed to be watching him. Then she apologizes and says it's not my fault. Ms. Wells tries to get her to drink something to help her calm down. The cops talk to her too, but she can't tell them anything.

After a while, I run to the bathroom and throw up. Then I get diarrhea and throw up again. I make sure there's no mess, so nobody has to know. If they see that my stomach is sick because I'm scared about Austin, then they'll just try to make me feel better, and that'll make me feel worse.

It's almost six o'clock when Ms. Wells comes over with a sandwich for me and one for Mom. Mom doesn't want to eat but tells me to. I'm not hungry, but I eat it anyway. It's dry and hard to swallow. She brought water too, but I'm too freaked out by seeing the red water in the sink to drink it yet. Why hasn't anybody come to talk to us about Austin yet?

I get up and walk back and forth in the waiting room. I see the doctors wheeling old people in wheelchairs, and some kids are screaming as the doctors try to ask them what's wrong. It's almost dark now, but I can still see the sun at the bottom of the sky through the doors outside.

Then I see the doctor walk out. I don't know why I know he's for us, but I just do.

Maybe it's the eyes. They're strong and blue and looking right at us. He's undoing his doctor cap and walking toward us. A nurse walks beside him. She looks young and nice.

I stand up and take a step to the doctor. As he gets closer, he looks more tired. Not tired like when I can't stay awake, but tired like he never goes home and is always here seeing people die.

Mom and Ms. Wells follow me and he stops in front of us and clears his throat. "I'm Dr. Paul North. You're Austin Palmer's family?"

Mom nods. "I'm his mom. Oh my God, is he—?" Her cries choke her.

He sighs. "He's alive. It was touch and go for a bit there, but he's alive." She nods and he eases her into a chair.

"Is he going to stay that way?"

Dr. North is quiet and looks down a moment before answering her. "I know how cliché it sounds to say that the next twenty-four hours are critical. You hear it on TV, and we say it so often, it must sound like we don't know what we're doing. But for Austin, that is how we have to move forward. I don't want to sugarcoat this. Your son was stabbed, and at his age, that's a serious injury. He's young and strong. This is something we can beat. But we have to monitor him closely for infection and any possible complications. Right now, Austin's going to need you all to be there for him. Take this one hour at a time."

Mom nods. "You said that you're treating him for infections. Do you have his records? He's allergic to some medicines."

He holds out his hand and points to me. "Your son told us. He was very brave when Austin was brought in. I understand he helped keep Austin alive on the way over."

Mom turns to me and pulls me into a hug. She kisses my head. "Can we see him?"

He signals to the nurse. "Yes, Judy here will take you to his room. She'll be taking care of him tonight. For tonight at least, let's keep it to two visitors at a time, though."

He turns to go but Mom stops him. "Thank you. Thank you for helping him."

"I'm just doing my job, ma'am."

"Do I need to know anything? What to look for? Anything?"

He nods. "Let's get you in to see him first. We'll talk about what to look for a little later."

Nurse Judy smiles and takes me by the hand. "He's still unconscious, but your brother is strong. He's fighting to stay with us."

Mom turns to Ms. Wells. "Thank you, Karen. I really appreciate you staying and doing all this."

"Where else would I be?"

"You should go home and get some rest. You have class tomorrow and your clothes . . ." She turns away and covers her face.

She takes Mom in her arms. "I'm not worried about any of that. I'm here for my friends."

Mom nods and takes me to follow Nurse Judy. Ms. Wells waits behind.

The halls are so long and pale. Hospitals always scare me. I haven't been in one since Dad died. It looks the same. I remember the tubes coming out of him and the machine that breathed for him, and I don't want to see Austin look like that.

We walk past an open room, where an old man is on a machine like that and is asleep. A woman is with him talking to him.

Mom nudges me on until we get to Austin's room. It's dim and a little cold.

There he is on the bed. He's not awake yet, but I can hear his heart monitor slowly beeping away. *Beep. Beep.* He doesn't have a tube down his throat like Dad did. Just a wire under his nose that gives him air. And he's got a weird device on his finger that glows.

Mom gently lifts up the covers. Austin only has on a hospital gown. What did they do with his clothes? I see the bandages under Austin's gown. They're so big for something a pair of scissors did.

Mom kisses his forehead. "Oh, my poor baby. I'm so sorry, Austin. Mommy should've been there sooner."

I want to go closer to hug him, but I feel my chest heavy. I'm scared to touch him like this. He almost looks asleep, but he looks so weak and he's not fussing like he usually does when he's sleeping. He's so pale too, even worse than when we all had the flu last year.

Mom turns to me. "You should go with Ms. Wells. Get cleaned up and get some sleep."

I shake my head. "I can't leave Austin. He's my brother."

"Austin's going to need his big brother when he

wakes up. And he's going to need you to be strong and not tired."

My lips tense and hot tears run down my cheeks. "I ain't going to school tomorrow. I'm coming back first thing in the morning."

She nods. "Of course. If he wakes up, I'll tell him you helped save him."

I cry harder. "I didn't save him at all. If I did, he wouldn't have gotten hurt."

Mom goes to kiss me goodnight, but I run away. Down the scary halls to where Ms. Wells is still waiting for me.

She hugs me tight. "Shhhh! It's going to be all right. I know it looks scary, but that's just how hospitals are. Let's get you out of here. You can crash at my place tonight."

I want to fight her, but I don't feel good enough to do it, so I let her walk me out.

Ms. Wells' house is smaller than I thought and very tan. Even the TV cabinet is tan.

"My son's bedroom is still made up for when he comes home. He won't be home from school for another few weeks, so you can sleep there tonight. Some of his old clothes should fit you."

I nod and set the backpacks down, Austin's and mine.

I go to the bathroom and wash my face, then change into one of her son's t-shirts.

It's big and comes down to my knees, but I don't care.

"Do you need anything? A glass of water or maybe something else to eat?"

I shake my head and climb into the bed. The sheets are softer and newer than the ones at home.

"Have a good night, Conner. If you need anything at any time, please don't hesitate to ask me."

I nod, and she closes the door all but a crack.

Twenty minutes of painful quiet. I don't know how to sleep without hearing Austin below me. I know he's safe at the hospital, but I can't sleep without him. Stop feeling sorry for yourself, Conner. Austin deserves better. But I don't know how to feel like anything's fine. I close my eyes and see Austin's blood all over me, and I just can't fall asleep now. What if I dream of it? What if I wake up and he's dead? He looked so helpless in that bed.

I scramble out of bed and down the hallway to the bathroom. I pull the seat up and try to pee, but only a little bit comes out. I haven't drunk anything but a sip of water all day. No wonder nothing's left. I flush anyway and wash my hands in the sink. I see myself looking back in the bathroom mirror. I look even more scared than I feel, and my eyes are still crying, even though I thought they stopped.

The doorbell rings. Who's visiting Ms. Wells this late?

I crawl down the hall and sit at the top of the stairs

and listen. I hear someone come in. I recognize the voice greeting her.

"I heard about Austin." Father Doyle. "Is he going to be okay?"

Ms. Wells starts crying. "I don't know . . . there was so much blood on the ground. And he's so small. The doctors say he's got a chance, but it could still go south. I'm scared, Father. Rose and Conner have already been through so much already. If he dies . . ."

"Let's not get ahead of ourselves. Austin's alive. Focus on that, and we can pray that whatever happens, we can all get through this. How's Conner?"

"How you'd expect. You know him, how he stews on things. He's shutting me out, and I don't know what to say. What can I say to a boy who had to stop his brother from bleeding to death with his own bare hands? No kid should have to go through that. And now he's in a strange bed, alone for the first time since he can remember. I want him to talk to me. It's healthy and he needs it. But I don't know how to make him talk to me, or even what I'd say if he did. How can I reassure a little boy when I can't even reassure myself?"

"Pray. At the end of the day, that's the most any of us can do. I'll be praying for all of you. And I'll make sure to pay Austin a visit as soon as he's able to have company."

"What about the school? What do we tell the children? The blood spot probably isn't even cleaned yet."

"It's roped off. They're still looking into what happened."

"They're all going to see that in the morning."

"The school won't open tomorrow. But after the weekend . . . we can't just ignore what happened. We need to talk to them about it. Maybe seeing it can be important. Remind them that we are all living beings, God's children. And when we hurt each other, the consequences are real and can be unpleasant. I think I'll schedule an assembly first thing on Monday, and we can talk to them. We'll have counselors available to answer questions and concerns."

"Do you need me there?"

"No. Stay with Rose and Conner. They're going to need all the support they can get."

Ms. Wells cries again.

I can't listen anymore. I run back to the bedroom and throw myself under the covers. It's hot, even with the AC. But I don't care. I don't want her to see me if she walks by, but I'm crying so much. The pillow underneath is soaked, but I can't stop it. I just want Austin to stay alive. Oh God, Austin, please don't die. Don't take my brother away. I repeat those words in my head over and over again and hope God will hear them. God already took my Dad away. He can't take Austin away too. I pray it again even though I'm starting to feel tired. I can't sleep if Austin's hurt. Again. Over and over . . .

Chapter 6
Austin

I feel my eyelids wiggling and hear a beeping sound in my ear. Like a heartbeat.

Is it mine? I open my eyes real slowly and look around. It looks like a hospital room. Like the one Daddy died in, but smaller and quieter. Why am I here?

My side stabs me, and I put my hand there and feel soft clothy stuff taped to the side of my belly. I look around and see Mommy looking at me with a smile.

"Look who's awake." She smiles and strokes my forehead. "How are you feeling?"

"Sleepy."

"You had a rough day. Do you remember what happened?"

I think back a minute. I remember my birthday party. And breakfast. And Robert.

He took my scissors. "Robert stabbed me with scissors."

Mommy's eyes go wide, and she takes my hand in hers. "We'll tell the police officers tomorrow. Tonight, you just rest and try to get better."

"Where's Conner?"

"Hopefully asleep at Ms. Wells' house."

"Did I die, Mommy?"

Mommy doesn't answer and starts crying. She kisses my forehead. "You're alive. You should get some more sleep so you can get strong and better. We can talk more in the morning."

I nod yes and try to fall asleep again where I can play with Conner and Daddy and nobody's hurt or being mean to me. Then I fall awake again when I hear Mommy talking.

The man looks like a doctor. I hear Mommy call him Dr. North. Then I hear my name, so I try to listen closer.

"It's very good that he's awake," Dr. North says. "Even better that he seems alert and his discomfort is befitting his injuries."

Mommy paces back and forth. "I don't like that tone. I feel like there's this big 'but' coming."

Dr. North looks Mommy in the eyes. "Austin didn't bleed to death in that hallway or on the way here. He didn't die on the table. These are good things. I know you are worried, but you have to focus on how far he's already come."

"That would be so much easier if you could put my mind at ease that he's out of the woods."

Dr. North gulps. "With injuries like this, there are still so many things that could go wrong."

"Are there signs I should look for? Something that

could indicate a complication?"

"You're his mother. Be that. That's what he needs most right now. You shouldn't be burdened with trying to decide what is normal and what you should be afraid of. We're monitoring him. If something does happen, somebody is on call at all times. With any luck, this night will go as smoothly as possible. If there is a complication, we'll do everything we can to fight it."

"You're talking about an infection, right?"

He nods. "The scissors made a tear in his peritoneum. Now, I was able to repair it, but any foreign object piercing the body leaves room for infection."

What's a peritoneum? I didn't even know I had one. Mommy doesn't know either and asks him.

"The peritoneum is the serous membrane lining the abdominal cavity. We stopped the bleeding, but with Austin being young and fragile, his immune system is very weak. The fact that he's allergic to several antibiotics also limits the options for preventing infection. But let's not get ahead of ourselves. Like I told you before, we'll take things as they come."

"There must be something I can do to help you monitor his progress."

Dr. North is quiet a minute. "This might sound crazy, but monitor his urine output. Since he's awake, we took out the catheter for the time being. There's a bottle in there with measurements. A nurse will be in to check periodically, so keeping tabs on that can tell us some very important things."

Why does Mommy have to check my pee? Why do the doctors care about that?

Mommy looks over and sees me watching. "The doctor used a lot of big words. Bet you're wondering what they mean."

I nod yes.

She kisses my forehead and smiles. "All you have to worry about is that the doctors are going to take such good care of you until you're all better."

"Can Conner see me tomorrow?"

Mommy nods and sits down beside my bed again. "I don't think I could keep him away, even if I wanted to. He's worried about you too, Austin."

"I'm sorry I couldn't fight back right."

"What do you mean?" Her eyes narrow on me.

"Conner said I needed to fight back against Robert so he would stop picking on me. I tried so hard. I thought maybe I did it, but it didn't work."

Mommy gets quiet, and I see that scared look on her face. Maybe I shouldn't have told her yet.

"My side hurts." I try not to cry, but the shooting pain is starting to get a little worse.

Mommy squeezes my hand. "The doctors are giving you medicine to help the pain. You went through a lot, honey. It's going to hurt until it heals more. Maybe something to eat will help you feel a little stronger."

I shake my head. "Not hungry."

"You should eat something. The doctors want you to go to the bathroom."

"I'm thirsty. They said the needle in my arm will give me water, but I don't think it works."

Mommy pours some water in a cup from a pitcher on the table.

I reach out to take it, but my hand feels so heavy. I can't keep it up or hold the cup.

"Mommy will help." She holds the cup to my mouth and turns it up so I can drink. I feel like a baby.

I drink the water and swallow, but some spills down my mouth and onto my hospital gown. All gone.

She puts the cup down and wipes my face. "Do you need to go to the bathroom?" I shake my head. "No. But if I do, you can't come. You're a girl."

Mommy laughs. "You're consistent, Austin. I'll give you that."

"What's consistent?"

She smiles. "Just tell me if you have to go. How 'bout a story for right now?"

"I don't want to hear about Austin being sick."

"Who says this story was about Austin?" She raises her eyebrow. "I know more than one story, you know. This story is about a boy named Kevin who went to the hospital after he got hurt."

"Did the doctors make him better?"

"Mhmm." She tickles my arm. "His mommy and

brother and teacher all were there to help him, and he got better and stronger, and it was like he never got hurt. Just like we're going to do with you."

"I have to go peepee." I look at the bottle on the table. "I can't go in that."

Mom picks up the bottle. "They want you to go in here, sweetie. They need to measure it to make sure."

I exhale hard. I don't like Mommy seeing my boypeer. Only Conner can see it because he has one too and is my brother. So he wouldn't try to hurt me. Conner used to say that girls can only pee in China, and that's why they take so long in the bathroom, because they have to crawl all the way through the pipes and back again to get to China's special machine that can suck the pee out. But boys can go fast because God needs them to get back to playing. I think Conner's lying, but I still don't like Mommy seeing me pee. No girls allowed.

"It was only a few years ago I was changing your diapers, you know."

"That was like five years ago. That was like forever."

She laughs and sits down next to me. "Austin, we're not fighting about this. If you have to go, I have to help."

I sigh and nod yes. I got no choice. I don't have my underwear, so we just pull up my hospital gown and put the bottle where I can pee into it. I go a little but can't go as much as I thought I could.

"I think I'm done," I say.

Mommy pulls it back and looks in the bottle. "That's not a lot . . ." She calls in Nurse Judy, and she writes stuff down on a chart. Then Mommy dumps it in the bathroom.

"I'm sleepy."

"Why don't you go back to sleep? Maybe you'll feel better in the morning."

"Okay." We kiss goodnight, and I close my eyes.

Dr. North comes in a few minutes later. Mommy thinks I'm still asleep, but I'm awake. And I can hear them. I keep my eyes closed, so they still think I'm asleep and don't try to not say things they think will scare me.

"How's he doing?" Dr. North's footsteps come close to me. I feel him touch my head and check things around me.

"Well, I'm not sure. He's complaining of a side ache. He was thirsty but didn't want to eat."

"Has he gone to the bathroom any yet?"

"A little."

Dr. North breathes deeply and paces.

"Doctor, you're scaring me. Is something the matter?"

"He had surgery today. Lack of appetite is understandable. And without eating, going to the bathroom isn't happening anyway."

"Why do you sound like you're trying to convince yourself more than me?"

"Let him sleep for right now. We'll run some tests

in the morning, when we have a better idea of where we stand."

"Doctor, is something wrong with my son? Is this one of the complications you warned me about?"

"Let's not play this game yet. If we know anything for sure, we will tell you. There's nothing to be gained from you losing sleep for something that probably isn't happening. Just be with him tonight. That's what he needs right now."

Mommy thanks Dr. North and he leaves.

Mommy comes back to my side, and I hear her crying. She prays to Jesus that I'll be okay and asks Mama Mary for me not to die. Am I going to die after all? I thought when I woke up after Robert killed me, it meant I wasn't going to die.

I listen to Mommy cry until she falls asleep.

Daddy and Conner play with me on the beach. Conner says I'm scared of the waves, but I ain't scared.

Conner says he'll prove it. He holds me upside down as a wave comes crashing onto us and knocks us down. But I don't mind. The water is cold and fun and I laugh.

Daddy picks me up and swings me. He calls my name and holds me steady as another wave comes.

This one hurts. My side is so sharp, like it's exploding. And I scream. It hurts so bad.

I rip my eyes open and scream for Mommy. "Mommy! Mommy!"

Mommy rushes to my side and feels my cheeks. "Austin? Austin, what's wrong?"

"It hurts. My side hurts so bad. Make it stop. Make it stop hurting."

Mommy runs into the halls and screams for help. "Something's wrong with my son. Get Dr. North. Or anybody. Just get somebody to help him."

She runs back to me and strokes my head. "Help's coming, Austin. Hold on." She feels my head and yanks her hand back. "You're burning up."

My breaths are heavy. "But I'm cold."

She feels my skin again and starts to cry. I'm crying too. Dr. North comes in with Nurse Judy.

Nurse Judy tries to hold me down. I try to wiggle out, but she pushes harder. "It hurts." Why can't they fix me? I look at Nurse Judy, and she looks scared. It's never good when doctors or nurses look scared.

"What's wrong with him?" Mommy's voice is loud. "I can't lose him. You have to help him."

"We're going to do everything we can, Mrs. Palmer. Please, step back. We're going to help him." Dr. North stands over me and starts looking me over and feeling me.

"Can't you stop the pain? I can't take him screaming."

I didn't even hear me screaming, but now I do. It hurts so much.

Dr. North points to Nurse Judy. "Get her out of here. She shouldn't need to see this."

Nurse Judy nods and takes Mom into the hall, but I see her looking in with her hands over her face.

Nurse Judy comes back, and Dr. North tells her to take my temperature.

"104."

"Christ . . ." Dr. North looks away. Is he trying to talk to Jesus? I feel me shaking now. It must be the cold and the pain.

"He's got the chills too."

"Doctor, what do you want to do?"

Dr. North says a bunch of medical stuff I don't understand. It all runs together like my train with the broken wheel used to.

Nurse Judy takes off my hospital gown. I'm even colder now, but it hurts too much to tell Nurse Judy she can't see me without clothes on.

Dr. North touches my side where Robert killed me with the scissors. It makes it hurt even more, and I scream louder. "I don't feel good." My stomach starts turning like when I had the virus last year.

"Austin?" Dr. North turns my head to him. "Do you feel like you have to throw up?"

I nod yes.

He grabs a pink square bucket from under the bed, but it's not fast enough. I cough throw up on him, and a lot squirts on me. This makes my side hurt even more, but I can't scream, and I just ask God to make it stop hurting.

Everything starts spinning, and I fall back. Dr.

North catches me from hitting the bed hard.

"I'm sorry," I say.

"That's okay, Austin. I got a hundred more just like it." He touches his doctor clothes.

"You're a nice doctor."

He smiles just a little but then looks to Nurse Judy. "Get him washed off. Cold water. Then we'll run some tests."

Nurse Judy picks me up and takes me to the bathroom in the room. There's a stand-up shower there but no tub under it like at home. She turns the water on. I can't stand, so she holds me under the shower water in her arms. It's so cold and I scream.

"It's okay, Austin."

Nurse Judy gets wet too, but she doesn't seem to be mad.

I want to tell her that she's a girl and she can't see me, but the cold makes it hurt just a little less. And I don't want to get in trouble.

When we're clean, she dries me off. I look and see my bandage wet. She takes it off, and I see my stab. It's so red and puffy.

Dr. North comes in and looks over my stab. Then they put new bandages and another hospital gown on me. They carry me back to the bed and hook me up to the water and the heartbeat machine again.

Mommy is back in the room. She's looking at her wallet picture of me and Conner wrestling. Conner won.

Nurse Judy pulls the covers over me and feels my head. "You're a great kid, Austin. We're going to make sure you stop hurting soon."

Mommy takes Nurse Judy aside. "I'm sorry about that outburst before."

Nurse Judy touches Mommy's shoulder. "It's okay, hun. You're not the first and won't be the last. You're his mother. It's your job to worry. It's our job to give you fewer reasons to."

"There must be so many other mothers here like me. Some here for so long and I don't know how they do it. One night and I'm already so weak and tired . . . how do mothers survive doing this for a long time? What if he doesn't get better?"

"It's never easy, but whatever happens, you'll get through. We're doing everything we can to help Austin. Hopefully soon you'll all get through this, and you can go back to getting him to do his homework."

I'm never doing homework again because I'm never going back to school again. You get killed there.

I feel sleepy again and close my eyes. I hear Mommy singing to me before I'm back at the beach with Daddy. Conner's not here now, but Daddy and I play and we have fun.

Chapter 7
Conner

As I roll awake, I reach down to wake Austin up for school. He's not there.

Where is he?

Wait, he's at the hospital. I remember. And now it hurts and I cry, but I stuff it up before Ms. Wells comes in and sees me.

I see clothes in my size on a chair in the room. They aren't mine, but I change into them anyway. They're cool and comfortable. I check my backpack again and find my wallet in the secret compartment nobody knows about, not even Mom. I pull the zipper and reach in and take out some money. It's only 7 dollars. Not much but maybe I can buy Austin something to make him happy.

Austin . . . is he even still alive? He could be dead by now for all I know. He was bleeding so much and looked so weak and sick in that hospital bed. If he died overnight, Ms. Wells wouldn't come in to tell me while I was asleep. I pull out a picture from the secret compartment too. Austin was 4 and I was 7. It was our last picture with Dad. Mom looked happier too. I was Austin's age now back then, but I looked older than he does.

He's so small sometimes. I know he remembers Dad, but I never can tell just how much. He was so young, but he cried so hard when he knew Dad wasn't coming home. I knew I had to be the man of the house after that and take care of him because he needed me.

Now he's alone and I can't do anything to help him.

I look at his backpack and pull it close to me. I hug it and try to feel like I'm hugging Austin. I open it up and see something sticking out of one of his folders. It's a cutout picture of him, me, and Mom. Dad's up in heaven. His drawing sucks, but it's so cute. What if this is the last thing he'll ever make? I put it away before more tears fall out. I don't want to get it wet.

I touch Austin's books. I try to feel close to him. Then I zip our bags up and push them away. Maybe Ms. Wells can take me to see him.

She's made pancakes when I get downstairs. Banana pancakes. The smell makes me think of Austin's shampoo.

"Good morning, Conner. I figured you could use a solid meal after everything yesterday."

I shrug. "I'm not really hungry, but thanks."

"Hey, you're not going to help yourself, or Austin, by starving yourself. Sit down." She pours me a glass of orange juice and puts two pancakes and a sausage stick on a plate.

I don't feel like fighting with her, so I sit down

and say a prayer before I start eating. She picks at a pancake but doesn't eat much.

"Can I see Austin today?"

She nods. "Yes. We'll take you. But I am going to stop at the school to pick up some of your books. You might be out for a while next week."

"I don't care." I move a piece of pancake around in the syrup on my plate. "Did you talk to Mom? Is Austin going to be okay?"

"Her phone's been off all night. I called the hospital, but they won't give me any updates. You know they have silly rules."

"Can we stop so I can buy Austin a present on the way?"

She smiles. "Of course. I know a great place nearby."

Mrs. Wells lets me sit up front because the back seat still has Austin's blood on it. She says she'll have to get it cleaned but makes an exception for me to sit up front today, if I wear my seatbelt.

After we pick up my books and put them in the trunk, we stop at a small strip of stores on a side street I don't remember seeing. There's a toy store on the edge that has trains on the sign.

Inside, there are all sorts of cool toys. Nothing like Disney toys but all unique stuff, like toy trains and helicopters.

"Wow, I've never been here before."

She smiles and walks me around. "There aren't many stores like these anymore. Everyone always wants the latest and the greatest, but I think there's something to be said for classics. So do you see anything you think Austin would like?"

I go through some of the aisles and touch the toys. Some are really expensive, but a few are cheap enough for me to buy. But I don't know if Austin would like those. A puzzle game would be too hard, and I'm not sure what he'd do with magnets.

Then I see a bin of stuffed animals in the corner of the store. Austin always likes stuffed animals. And they aren't too expensive, so maybe I can get him one of these. I dig through the bin and see which one Austin would like best. A lot of them are pink and girly, like unicorns and girl dolls or puppies with ribbons on their head. Bleh.

Near the bottom, I see something red. It's a parrot. I think it's a macaw. I remember Austin's birthday when he said he wanted a parrot. Maybe it's not real, but it's the best I can do since real parrots cost a lot of money.

"Do you think he'd like this?"

Ms. Wells smiles and nods. "I think he'd love it." I check the price tag. $9.99. Darn. I can't afford it.

Ms. Wells looks over my shoulder. "How much did you bring?"

"7 . . ."

She reaches into her wallet. "How about I loan you the difference, and you can pay me back later?"

"I don't get that much money."

"We'll figure out something. But let's worry about that later." I smile and clutch the parrot close. Austin's going to love it.

We go to the cashier and he checks us out. I tell him it's for my brother in the hospital, and he says he hopes my brother feels better soon.

As we drive to the hospital, Ms. Wells sees me holding the parrot close. "That was very nice of you to buy him a present, Conner. I'm sure he's going to love it."

I stare out the window. We pass the playground where we had Austin's party.

Nobody's there yet. Maybe I should've played more with Austin.

"You're a good brother." Ms. Wells must see my face. "Austin loves you more than anything. He talks about you every day. If I didn't know you well already, I'd know you inside and out, just from what Austin tells me every day."

"I didn't keep him safe. How did he get stabbed? Did Robert do it? Robert's the only one who hates Austin enough to stab him."

Ms. Wells swallows hard and turns into the hospital parking garage. "I don't know what happened, but we'll let the police handle that. Right now, we have to focus on making Austin better. And you buying him a present sure helps with that."

Yeah right. She knows what happened and is too scared to admit that one of her students hurt another one. If I ever see Robert again, I'm making him pay.

As we walk to the hospital, I see Father Doyle coming from the other way. I don't know how he can wear his cassock when it's so hot out.

"I was hoping I could see them today. I figured Rose could use all the support she could get."

Ms. Wells shakes his hand. "Thank you for coming. She'll appreciate it. Austin will like seeing you too."

He takes me aside. "What's that you got there?"

I look down. "I bought Austin a present."

He smiles. "That's very thoughtful of you. It's a sign of how good a brother you are that you're giving of yourself to make him happy."

We go into the elevator. Austin loves elevators because he likes the buttons and going up and down, but they always make me scared. I get woozy feeling the floor vibrate. And what if we get stuck and nobody gets us out? What if Austin dies while I'm stuck in an elevator? Then he'll never get to have his present.

Bing.

The doors open and we step out. I march ahead and then freeze. I don't remember where Austin's room is, and this place is so big. I can see out a big window that we're in the middle of the hospital. Even though we aren't high up, and I can still see pretty far. I didn't even look last night.

Ms. Wells touches my shoulder a moment. I feel her hands shaking. "His room's just down this hall," she says.

The hall seems so long, like we'll never get to his room. I'm afraid to see him. What if he's worse or dead? Oh please, God, let him be okay.

When I look up, we're outside his room.

As we go in to the room, everything seems normal. Austin is asleep. So is Mom.

His heart is still beating.

I run to Mom and wake her up.

She throws her arms around me and pulls me close. She doesn't say anything, but she doesn't have to.

"I bought Austin a present." I show her the bag.

She smiles and kisses my head. "That was so nice of you, Conner. Austin will love it."

I look over at him. "Did he ever wake up?"

She nods. "He was asking for you. He's just really tired from all that happened to him."

Ms. Wells walks to Mom and hugs her. "How is he? Do you know anything?"

Mom shakes her head. "Austin didn't really have a good night. I was scared for a minute, but they upped his medicine and it seems to be helping at least to keep him comfortable. Dr. North hasn't been back for a few hours now . . . I'm scared, Karen."

She hugs Mom tighter. "It'll be okay. Just keep praying."

Father Doyle walks in closer. "I hope you don't mind if I pop in."

"No, of course not." She walks to him and hugs him. "Austin loves you. He'll be so happy to see you."

"I can come back if he's resting. I don't want to disturb him."

Dr. North walks in. He waves Mom over. "Can we talk alone a moment?"

She fights tears. "Just tell me. Is he going to be okay? Is Austin going to live?"

"I don't think it's best to discuss these matters in front of everyone, especially the boys. There's an empty room just down the hall. We can talk there."

Father Doyle steps between them. "How about if I come with her, so she's not alone?"

Dr. North nods and leads Father Doyle and Mom out of the room. Austin will be okay with Ms. Wells. I follow Mom out.

Ms. Wells grabs me by the shoulder. "I don't think you should eavesdrop, Conner."

I break away and follow down the hall. I stop outside the room he takes Mom to so she doesn't see me.

"You called me away from them. That can't be good news." I hear her start crying. "Just tell me the truth. Is my baby dying?"

Dr. North sighs. "I brought up peritonitis before. Our latest tests confirm that Austin's developed this . . . it's an infection. A bad one. While not the only cause, it's not uncommon for abdominal traumas like stabbings to cause this to develop. Peritonitis is an inflammation of the peritoneum. Like I mentioned, the peritoneum is the thin membrane that covers the abdominal walls and covers the organs within. Peritonitis is often caused by something that allows bacteria, bile, or enzymes into the peritoneum through something like a hole or a tear in the gastrointestinal or biliary tracts."

Mom takes a deep breath. "This is all foreign to me, Doctor. I don't understand."

"When your son was stabbed with the scissors, they missed vital organs, but they made a tear in his peritoneum. We repaired the tear, but an open wound exposed at all increases risk of infections. Any time there's a puncture wound, infection is a common complication. We've been treating him with what antibiotics we can, but they don't seem to be working."

"So the pains he was feeling, the chills, they were all symptoms of this?"

Dr. North is silent a minute. "I didn't want to alarm you until I was sure. I didn't like what I was seeing—the thirst, the limited excretory functions, the symptoms you mentioned. So many things can cause a symptom that I wanted to have a definitive diagnosis before . . . giving you news like this."

I hear Father Doyle console Mom as she cries. After a minute, she gets herself together. "So what do we do? Can we still beat this? Can Austin still . . . is he going to die?"

Dr. North is quiet. And I don't like him being

quiet. I run away as tears spill out. I don't want Mom to know I listened in.

I run back to Austin's room and try to dry my eyes before Ms. Wells sees. As I walk in, I see Austin waking up.

He sees me first. "Conner! I missed you."

I walk over and sit on his bed. "No you didn't." I stick out my tongue. "You probably like having Mom all to yourself."

"I don't like peeing in a bottle with Mom holding it."

I chuckle. "Poor Austin."

"Ms. Wells." Austin smiles at her. "You came too. You carried me here."

She laughs. "Well, I carried you from my car. How are you feeling?"

"I'm still cold, but the doctors say the medicine is helping me not hurt so much. Did you find Robert?"

My chest starts burning. I knew that jerk was the one who hurt my little brother.

Ms. Wells shakes her head. "I can't get the police to tell me anything. I don't know what they're doing."

"Robert's dad is an important jerk," I say. "He probably forced the cops to pretend like they don't know who Robert is."

"But if Robert hurt me, don't they have to get him in trouble so he doesn't do it again?"

Ms. Wells looks away. "I don't know, Austin. I'm not sure what we can do. Don't worry about him. You focus on getting better."

"That's right." I grab the bag with the toy and give it to Austin. "I got you a present."

"For me? But my birthday was Wednesday."

"It's a get-well present."

He takes the present but can't seem to get it open. His hands look like they can barely move, so I help him.

We pull out the stuffed parrot. His eyes light up. "You got me a parrot."

"Well, it's just a toy."

"He's my favorite. He's so cute and cool. I'm gonna name him Pete!"

"That's a great name." I grab Austin's hand and squeeze a little. I can feel how weak he is by how he can't squeeze back. "You really like it?" I remember Dr. North's words and they sting me.

"I love it. He's perfect."

I hug Austin. He tries to hug me back but isn't strong enough. I try not to let him see me crying. I don't want him to be scared.

"I thought you thought a bird was lame." Austin looks me in the eyes. "I changed your mind." He can still smile at me.

Austin tries to move the parrot under his arm, but he can't, so I help him. He cuddles it close.

"You scared me, Austin."

"You're never scared. You're Conner. You're brave."

I shake my head. He's the brave one. Even if he's a

little scardeycat, he's still braver than me.

"Pete and me are going to take a nap again." Austin slips off to sleep before I can even say another word. He's barely been up a few minutes. He must be so hurt to need to sleep again.

Dr. North's words echo in my head, and I am scared Austin might not wake up soon.

Austin wakes up again when Mom comes in. I try to read her face, but she's hiding it well. She's even smiling.

"Hey, honey." She goes over to kiss Austin. "Is that what Conner bought you?"

He hugs it tighter and nods. "His name is Pete. I love him." She smiles and looks at me. "It's wonderful, Conner."

"Can we get a real parrot like Pete?" Austin looks up at her.

"Parrots are big and expensive. I think you'd better stick to Pete for now."

"But cockatiels are small and not expensive. They sit on your fingers and have cool hair and goofy cheeks."

Mom kisses Austin to try and not cry. "We'll talk about it later, Austin. When you're better."

"Okay." He sighs, and for a second, I see the not-sick Austin in there.

We don't leave Austin's room all day.

Father Doyle blesses Austin and then has to leave.

Ms. Wells brings us food and stays with us until it gets dark. Mom asks Ms. Wells to watch me another night, but I talk her into letting me stay with Austin tonight. The hospital says it's okay, even if it's against the rules.

I do my homework when Austin is asleep and talk to him when he's awake. I try to make Pete talk without moving my lips, but it's too hard, and I'm not very good at it.

Dr. North and Nurse Judy come in to check on Austin a lot throughout the day. They take his temperature and monitor how much he's peed. I didn't realize they had to stick a tube up him to take the pee out, but I guess it keeps him from having to keep going in a bottle or getting out of bed. I wish they looked happier. Every time they come in, they get more serious, and I get more scared.

Mom doesn't seem to know what to feel. She's trying so hard not to scare me or Austin, but what Dr. North told her must be bugging her. I see the same look in her eyes that she had when they told her that Dad wasn't ever going to wake up, and that she should take him off the machines. I hope Austin doesn't have to go on any more machines. Having a tube down your throat must hurt a lot.

Austin is trying to not look scared too, but I see the strength he usually has going away. And as the day goes on, something in his eyes goes dimmer and dimmer. I try to tell myself it's just in my head, but I'm so scared of hearing that beeping turn into a loud screech that takes Austin away forever.

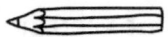

Austin's scream cuts through the quiet at midnight. Nurse Judy is at his side before Mom and I can even get up from where we were sleeping.

"I feel so sick." Austin's voice is barely louder than a whisper.

Austin gags and Nurse Judy quickly grabs a basin for him to throw up in. She steadies his head down so he doesn't get any on himself like he told me he did last night.

She pages Dr. North, who is there in barely a minute.

Austin is shaking again and can barely look up at Dr. North.

He reaches under Austin's robe and feels where Robert stabbed him. He shakes his head and says a curse word in a whisper.

Nurse Judy stares him down. "How bad are we talking, Doctor?"

He looks at Austin's charts. "Try upping the dosage again. It's all we can do. He's just not responding. His body can't take much more of this."

"Can we operate?"

"I don't think the infection is localized anymore. It's spreading too fast."

I try to go to Austin. "What's wrong with my

brother?"

Dr. North turns to me and moves me back. "We're doing everything we can." Doctors always say that when something bad is gonna happen. "Just stay back. That's how you can help Austin right now."

I'm not helping Austin. He's squirming in pain. Nothing anybody is doing is helping him.

Chapter 8
Conner

The sun's down now, and Austin's asleep again. They had to give him more drugs to make him hurt less.

Mom's been watching him for over an hour now, just stroking his head over and over.

I try to remember why I was so annoyed with him all the time. I always wanted to be left alone or not do what he wanted. But I know I loved him. So why did I treat him so bad? And why did he still love me, even though I was so mean to him?

Dr. North comes in. I can see it on his face. I know what he's going to say. He calls Mom out of the room again.

As she stands up, I can see it in her face. She knows too.

Mom closes the door behind her so I won't hear. Good. That makes it easier for me to hide behind it and listen close.

"He's dying, isn't he?" Mom's voice is deep and slow.

Dr. North doesn't answer right away. "The infection is spreading. He's showing signs of sepsis ... other organs are beginning to shut down . . . I know you're a woman of faith, and I don't want to discount the possibility of a miracle. We're doing everything we can . . . and I keep telling you that. And it's true, but it's not enough. The medicine isn't working, and if something doesn't change, we're going to lose him."

I open the door just a crack and peek out.

Mom is tensing her lips, trying not to cry. "How long? How long does he have?"

Dr. North paces a moment. "It depends how quickly the infection spreads. It could be tonight . . ."

"You're telling me my baby could die tonight?"

"I'm afraid there's a strong possibility. He could hang on a day or so, but you should prepare yourself. Prepare Conner . . . Austin. You should all be ready."

"How do I tell my little boy that he's going to die? Two days ago, we were celebrating him turning 7. How do I tell him now that he's going to stop being alive? I don't know if he's ready. And Conner? He loves his brother so much. They're not ready. I can't do this to them."

"I think both of them are a lot stronger than you realize. In the end, them being ready for this before it happens will keep you together better than letting them not know until it happens. But we do have things we need to discuss, about what to do if his heart stops . . ."

Tears rush out of me. I can't stay here. I won't hear them talk about letting Austin die.

I bolt out the door and down the hall. Mom calls out for me to stop, but I keep running because I can't look at her. I can't watch Austin die. He's my brother, and he's supposed to grow up with me.

I take the elevator to the ground floor. It moves even slower than usual. I know it doesn't have a mind of its own, but it feels like it wants to keep me trapped inside forever, so Austin dies without me.

I try to run out the door, but Security is waiting for me. Dr. North must've told them. They try to grab me, but I run the other way. I take the stairs back up to Austin's floor, but I can't go back and face Austin.

Dr. North sees me and tries to talk to me.

"No! I don't want to hear about Austin dying." I hold my ears and run down the hall. I don't know where. Anywhere but here.

I bump into somebody.

I open my eyes and see an older boy in his teens with hair that's red and brown. His eyes are a warm blue and a weird mix of happy and sad. He reaches down and helps me up. "Careful. You don't want to get hurt. Even if you are in a hospital, it'll still suck."

"Sorry about bumping into you." I try to wipe my tears so he doesn't see. "I wasn't paying attention."

"Hey, you okay?" He looks me over and tries to see into my eyes. "You look like you need to talk to someone. My name's Patrick. I'm good at listening."

I shake my head. Patrick seems nice, but there's no need to bug him with my crying. "I'm fine. You don't have to worry about me."

I go to run away, but he stops me.

"I've seen that look in your eyes before. In mine, in other people. You don't have to talk to me, but you should talk to someone. Whatever you're going through, you shouldn't try to do it alone."

I turn to him. His eyes look so full of care. Why? He doesn't even know me. "My brother's going to die. When he's dead, I'll be alone. Talking about it won't make me not alone." I continue to run down the hall.

When I stop to catch my breath, I'm back outside Austin's room.

I see Mom and we stare a minute. I sit down on the floor outside the room.

Mom talks to somebody. I think it's the nurse for a second, until I realize she's talking to Austin. He's not awake, but he probably still is listening because that's what he does. I turn in to look at them. Poor Austin. He looks worse now.

"You know, when you were born, you came out screaming. Didn't even need the smack on the butt. And then you were talking in your own little baby language at just a month or so. You were always running around, so full of energy and spirit. And you sang. You loved to sing. I figured you'd be some kind of singer when you grew up. Some days I saw myself going to Carnegie Hall to watch you perform some classic opera set, and others, it was a huge rock concert at a big sports arena with fire and screaming fans. You don't sing as much now, but I knew whatever you decided to do . . . you'd be great. You'd make a difference, singer, doctor, lawyer, pet psychologist." She chuckles and takes Austin's hand. "No matter what, there would be people gathered around, just for you. Because of you, because of Austin, their lives would be a little bit better." She cries harder. "Oh, Austin, I don't know what to do. I want you here with Mommy and Conner, but I don't want you to be in pain if you can't fight this. I don't know what to do, honey."

"Mommy . . ." Austin looks up at her. "Why are you crying?"

Mom tries to stuff her tears back in. She holds Austin's face, which looks wet and clammy even from all the way over here. "I'm just thinking about when you were a baby."

"Can I have Pete?"

"Of course." She grabs Pete from a table and tucks it under Austin's arm. He can't even raise his hands as high as earlier.

"Mommy, I can't move good."

"Does your side hurt less? The doctors are trying to make your pain stop."

"I just feel so sleepy, even after I sleep."

She kisses Austin's head. "I know. You'll be better soon." She squeezes his hand. "You won't hurt anymore."

I run back to the waiting area again. I don't want to

think about Austin being dead. He's not supposed to be dead. He's a kid, like me. We're supposed to play and go to school. We're not supposed to get stabbed or get bad infections or die.

I sink into a chair and try to hide my crying so nobody comes to ask me what's wrong. I feel so heavy now, and I close my eyes just a minute, trying to pretend Austin and I are at the playground again. Just him and me, trying to swing higher. No Robert. No dying. Just us.

The elevator doors wake me up. It's morning, but the sun is bright in my face. So it must still be really early.

I look down and see a cover on me. Did Mom leave it there? Or one of the nurses?

Ms. Wells and Father Doyle step off the elevator and see me. I see Father Doyle whisper something to Ms. Wells. She walks down the hall to Austin's room, looking worried. He walks over and takes a seat next to me.

"How are you doing, Conner?"

I pull the cover off and try to fold it, but it looks like a big clump. "Austin's gonna die." I can't believe I just said it. I look up at him, and he doesn't look surprised. Did he know already?

"I asked how you were doing."

"Who cares?"

"I care. I'm sure Austin would too."

"My brother's going to die and there's nothing I can do to help him. That's how I am. I love him so much, and God's going to take him away from me forever." I can't fight crying anymore.

Father Doyle reaches over and hugs me.

"Is God mad at me? Was I bad? I'm the one who told Austin to fight back against Robert. First Dad died, and now, Austin probably will too. Is God punishing me by taking Austin away?"

"No. God doesn't do that. What happened was . . . Robert did something wrong and Austin was hurt, and his body just can't survive it anymore. It's not your fault, and it's not God trying to punish you. It's just a consequence of our fallen world, and it's not something we can always understand. But Austin's soul isn't dying. No matter what happens, you and Austin are still brothers, and will be forever."

"I thought I was praying so hard for Austin to get better, but he's going to die anyway."

"I told everybody at Church about Austin. They're all praying for him. They all love him."

"Then why isn't it working?" I look up at him, at Jesus on a cross around his neck. "Why isn't God making Austin better?"

"I don't know. Sometimes we don't always know the answers, and it's not easy to just accept that. I've seen so many bad things . . . so many people die. They were good people. They were mommies and daddies, even children like you and Austin. I had to question my faith every day, but then I remembered all the good things I'd seen. The friendships, the selfless sacrifices, the love. For every bad thing I saw, I saw good things. And I had to remember that all the bad things were temporary. All the good things, the really good things, those things could stay forever, if we just wait. In heaven, all of the bad things are gone, and only the good things are left. And it might hurt, and you might cry when some of those good things go away from life here, and that's okay. It's okay to feel sad and to cry. But there's something that should comfort us when everything feels sad. God's got a place for all the good things to stay alive forever. No matter how much it feels like Austin is gone forever, he's not. It might feel like a long time away until you can see him again, but forever never ends. And when you see him again in heaven, it'll be like you never were apart. So when we don't know why something bad happens, that's okay. We just need to trust that even though it hurts now, in the end, all the hurt will go away."

"But I want the hurt to go away now. I want Austin to get better. Maybe God just wants Austin to die. Maybe I'm not supposed to be happy."

Father Doyle hugs me tighter. "God didn't stab Austin. He built a strong, beautiful boy, and he gave him a strong and loving brother to take care of him. Somebody else made a choice that caused that boy's body to be broken. God's just respecting that choice because He gives all of us the choice to be good or bad. At any moment, we can choose Him or choose to go against Him. And when we choose to go against Him, we hurt people. God doesn't want Austin to die now, but if Austin is going to die now, He's ready to take him to his forever home. He'll take all of us one day, if we choose to stay with Him. It's so hard to accept now when you have to go on living without someone. But if we're going to ask why, we have to be ready to accept the answers, even if we don't like them."

I break out of his hug and stand up. I know he's right, but Austin is dying. And right now I'm mad at God and Robert. We're not supposed to go to heaven until we're old. It's not fair that Austin has to die.

"Austin needs you right now."

I stop running and make a fist. "I can't make him not die."

"He's scared. Even people who are ready are scared. He needs everyone who loves him to help him through this. He needs his big brother."

"What can I do if he's going to die anyway?" Tears are everywhere now. I hate anybody seeing me cry like this, but I don't know how to stop them. They're just spilling out of me like rain.

"Pray for him. Now, after he dies, forever. Because then you'll always be holding his hand in spirit, even after you can't hold his physical hand anymore. Go be with him, and let him know that you love him. He knows, but hearing it again and again, that's what will help carry him through."

I walk away without saying anything else. I can't win a fight with a priest, and I don't want to stop being mad or sad or scared unless Austin gets better. I run down the hall to his room, but I'm too scared to go inside because I know the next time I go in, I won't be coming out until Austin's dead.

Chapter 9
Austin

I open my eyes and see Conner walking in. He's trying not to look sad, but I can see that he is. He hugs Mommy and Ms. Wells and asks them if he can talk to me alone for a minute. Mommy doesn't want to, but Ms. Wells talks her into it and they walk out.

Conner sits on the edge of my bed. "You look like you need a shower." He tries to smile, but it looks fake. Then he says I look like a word Mommy doesn't let me say.

I try to laugh, but I can only smile just a little. "You said a bad word."

"Only a little bad one." Conner gulps and moves closer. "You feeling better yet?"

I don't want to scare him, so I try to think of an answer that isn't a lie but doesn't make him cry. "The medicine makes it hurt less."

"That's good." A tear rolls down his face. I did it wrong.

I look into his eyes and see that he knows something bad but doesn't want to tell me. Mommy and Ms. Wells and the doctors all have that same look.

"Conner, am I going to die?"

Conner looks down, and more tears come out. "Why are you asking me? I'm not the doctor."

"They won't tell me. I feel it in my heart." I pat my chest. "Something is wrong inside." I'm crying too now. "I don't want to die, Conner, but I don't want to die by surprise because I want to make sure I kiss you and Mommy goodbye so you don't have to be sad about not saying goodbye like with Daddy."

Conner lays down his head on my chest. "Austin, you're crazy."

"Don't lie."

Conner looks up at me and nods yes. "They say the medicine isn't working anymore. They say germs got into your stab, and they're going to kill you. You're going to die, forever die. Not like when we pretend die at home but like Dad dying dead. Can't come back to life ever dying. And I don't want you to die, Austin. I don't know what to do because I really don't want you to die."

"I don't want to die. But maybe I get to see Daddy again."

"I want you to stay with me. Maybe if you fight really hard, you can show the doctors they're wrong."

I shake my head. "I don't know how to fight dying. I'm scared, Conner."

Conner holds my hand tight. "Me too."

"Are they gonna take my clothes off when I die like on TV and put me in a drawer like we put our shirts away in?"

"You're silly."

"But girls aren't supposed to see me without clothes."

Conner laughs, but he's still crying. "You'll be dead. You won't care."

"I don't know how it works. Will I still be me in my body when my soul isn't there? Will you come and see me and tell me it's okay?"

Conner hugs me.

I try to hug him back, but I can't.

"I'll always make sure you're safe, even after . . ."

"I'll try to talk to you from heaven, if Jesus lets me."

Conner squeezes me tighter. "I don't want you to die. Austin, I'm sorry I was a bad big brother. I failed. You're dying because I told you to fight back."

Conner's wrong. He's the best big brother in the world. "Robert did it, not you."

"If I didn't tell you to fight back, then you'd be okay. I should've just beat him up and kept you safe. I'm sorry I didn't want to take baths anymore, or that I yelled at you or didn't share enough. I was a bad brother, and now you're going to die. And I'll be alone forever. I won't have a brother anymore."

"We'll always be brothers, even if I'm with Jesus. Promise."

Conner doesn't say anything, but I hope he believes me because I don't want him to be sad because he misses me.

"Can you stay with me?"

Conner nods yes and crawls up next to me so our faces touch. His face is warm but slips on my skin a little. I like feeling his face next to me because it makes me feel safe.

I feel my insides stopping a little. I don't think there's a lot of time left until they don't work at all anymore.

Father Doyle comes in and waves to me. Mommy hugs him, and he says that he knows. He holds her while she cries, and then she walks out of the room.

I turn to Conner and ask him if I could talk to Father Doyle by myself. He says he'll go to the bathroom, but that he isn't going back into the hall. I tell him okay, and he gets up.

Father Doyle sits in the bed and smiles. "They tell me you've been a very brave little boy, Austin."

"I don't feel brave. I'm scared to die. Can you forgive that?"

"You mean like confession?"

"I know we're not in a booth like at Church, but maybe it can work here?"

He takes out a purple scarf from his pocket and puts it over his shoulders. "I'd be happy to hear your confession, but I will say that being scared to die isn't a sin, Austin. You're a little boy dealing with something very scary, and you're handling it better than many adults I've seen. Being brave doesn't mean not being scared. It means being scared and facing it anyway.

That's you, Austin."

"I've been bad sometimes." I try to think of all the times I didn't do what Mommy said or was mean to Conner and tell him. I hope I don't forget anything. "I kicked Robert in his boy parts so he'd leave me alone." I tell him about the time I tried to run away from home after Daddy died. I tell him about telling Mommy to go away when I was in the tub with Conner. I even tell him about a time I told Mommy I was bored during Church. I didn't want to hurt Jesus' feelings.

He listens and nods along without saying anything until I'm done.

"I'm sorry I wasn't good."

He reaches to my face and touches it. "God loves us, Austin. Even if we're not perfect. Being sorry when we do something wrong, and trying to change, is a sign that we're on the right path."

"Do you have to give me a prayer to say? Conner says you usually give a lot of prayers, like a whole ten beads of the rosary."

He laughs and takes my hand. "How about you just tell God that if you're hurting right now, maybe he could make another little boy or girl hurt less. God loves it when we give Him gifts like that. Is that okay?"

I nod and say, "God, make my pain make another kid feel better." I mean it too. I hope God lets me see the kid I helped.

He prays over me and makes the Sign of the Cross over me and tells me that I'm forgiven now. "I have something else for you." He takes out a little case and opens it up. He shows me a Jesus host.

"Jesus." I smile and am able to sit up a little. "But I'm not in the white suit. And I didn't go to the classes or practice."

"Right now, I think you're more ready than any of the kids receiving that sacrament in a few hours." He puts it to my lips. "Is this what you want?"

I nod yes and open my mouth. "The Body of Christ," he says.

"Amen."

He puts Jesus on my tongue, and I close my mouth, and it starts to melt. It doesn't taste like regular bread, but I know Jesus is in me now. He puts his hand on my head, and I see a tear in his eyes. I pray that Jesus lets him help other kids for a long time because he's really good at it.

Father Doyle takes out another small case. "I have another Sacrament I want to give you. It's called Anointing of the Sick. Do you know that one, Austin?"

"We studied it in school, but I thought that was only for old people."

He shakes his head. "It's for anybody who might die and needs some extra help from God."

"How does it work?"

"Let me show you." He puts his thumb in the oil, and then makes a cross on my forehead. "Through this holy anointing, may the Lord in His love and mercy help you with the grace of the Holy Spirit." He unfolds my hands and makes a cross on each one. "May the Lord who frees you from sin save you and raise you up. Amen."

"Amen," I say. "Is that all?"

He nods. "It helps people who are dying, even little boys."

"I don't feel as scared now. I'm still scared but not as much."

He smiles and folds my hands together. "Pray for us when you see Jesus, Austin. Because of you, I think we've all had our lives enriched. You're a good kid, Austin. I think God's going to use you to make a lot of good happen, even when you're in heaven."

"What's heaven like? What does my soul look like? Does it look like my face? I know we turn into bones after we die, and they have to bury us so we don't stink. I saw that on TV. But nobody talks about heaven much. Just that it's happy and in the sky, and everyone wears white and has a halo."

"We don't know what it's like. I think God wants us to love Him from what we see here. Heaven is seeing Him and everyone we love with all of the bad things about earth gone and all of the good things made bigger. You are a body and a soul, and one day, you'll get your body back. And it won't be hurt anymore. I don't know what a soul will look like, but everyone you love will still know who you are, and you will know who they are."

"That's cool." I smile and lay back down again.

Sitting up makes me dizzy. "Am I the only kid you know who's ever died?"

He shakes his head. "Too many . . . there was a boy just about your age. Tommy. He had leukemia. That's a type of cancer in the blood."

"Where you lose your hair?"

"The medicine made that happen. He wore a baseball cap to hide it. He didn't have any brothers or sisters and was scared to leave his mommy and daddy alone, but I told him he could still watch over them with Jesus in heaven. You can do the same to your brother and mother too. There was another kid. He was about 13. His name was Ryan. His dad was a bad man, and he hurt a lot of people. But Ryan didn't like seeing people hurt. When his dad tried to hurt one of Ryan's friends, Ryan got in the way, and he died . . . He saved his friend's life. There were so many, and it doesn't stop being sad. But I guess I hope every day that all of you are up there in heaven waiting for us and praying for us."

"I'll pray for you every day in heaven. Do you think I'll see them up there? What if they're on the other side the whole time? Heaven's real big, you know. And maybe I won't know them."

"Heaven's not like here. There's no other side. Everywhere is like here, and here is everywhere. You'll know everybody, and they'll know you."

"Will I still be a kid in heaven?"

"In heaven, there's no big or little. There's just you."

I smile and try to picture what heaven looks like. I picture a big place above the sun and moon and stars, with Jesus in the middle, and all the angels and good people around Him happy. And Mary there bringing everybody up to see Him. "It must be so great . . ."

He hugs me and gets up to go. "It will be. God be with you, Austin. Always and forever."

"And with your spirit," I say like at Church.

He laughs but is crying too. Everyone is doing that today. He waves goodbye as he walks out. I try to wave back, but my hand is so heavy. I feel dizzy again, and my eyes close. I think I'm dead at first, until I see Conner and me swimming in a bowl of milk with huge fruit loop floats. Then I know it's just a dream, and I'm not dead yet.

Chapter 10
Conner

The clouds swallow the sun in the afternoon. I know sun won't make me feel better about Austin dying, but the clouds make me feel worse.

I look over to him. He's sleeping again. He's probably going to be dead in a few hours, and he can barely even stay awake to spend them with us.

Mom talks to him and tells him stories, even when he's asleep.

Ms. Wells knocks and comes in. "I brought you something to eat." She sets down two juices and two dinners on a table.

"Thanks," Mom says without even looking at them. Ms. Wells brings mine to me. "You should eat."

"Austin should be not dying."

She sits down next to me on the windowsill. "I know you're in pain, Conner, but I thought we went over this. You're not going to help Austin by going hungry."

"He's dying right over there. How can I eat anything?"

She's quiet. She can't come back to that.

I hop up from the seat and pace. I don't know what

to do. I don't want to leave, but I can't just stand here and watch him slowly die. And lying next to him and feeling his breathing slow down hurts more.

Dr. North comes in and checks Austin's vitals. "It won't be long now," he says. "Are you sure about what we discussed earlier?"

Mom nods. "I don't want to put him through that. If we can't beat the infection, I don't want to drag out his suffering just so I have him with me a little bit longer. If his body can't take it, let him be at peace." She cries again.

I look down so I don't shoot the doctor my evil eye. Why can't they fight harder for Austin? They seem to be just giving up, but what if them fighting is what would save him?

"I'll be back in a bit to check up again." He pats Austin's arm and walks out. He must be used to this by now. He probably sees kids die every day. Austin's just another case to him.

"I had a sister," Ms. Wells says. She touches my shoulder. "Her name was Therese."

"Why are you telling me this?"

"I know you think that nobody can know what you're feeling right now, but we all lose somebody sooner or later. I wasn't as young as you when she died. I was grown. In fact, it was the year you were in my class. You remember when I had to go away for a few weeks?"

I nod. "We had a lot of subs. They weren't as good

as you."

"I needed that time to get together because I went through a lot of the same feelings you are right now. I know being a kid, this is all so much scarier for you. But no matter how old you are, you're never ready to see somebody you love die."

My stomach turns more, and the acid feeling returns. I don't like thinking about this or talking about it. "Was she sick? Or did somebody hurt her like Robert hurt Austin?"

Ms. Wells pulls me into a hug. "She was missing for a couple of years. We didn't know if she was alive or dead, or even if she ran away or was kidnapped. My mom and stepfather—her dad—hired this man to help find her and he was wonderful. He was so dedicated to finding her. Even after we gave up, he wouldn't give up the case. And a few years ago, he finally solved it. She was being held with a lot of other people by a very bad man. Unfortunately, by the time the police got there, he'd already killed her."

"I'm sorry. I didn't know."

"I don't like to talk about it. But for three years, I was like you are now. I had hope that it would all turn out okay, or it would if we just tried a little bit harder. But another part of me knew that I wouldn't ever see her alive again. When I saw her body, she looked peaceful. But I knew she died afraid, and I wasn't there. I kept telling myself she'd still be alive if I just did this differently or that. But it wasn't my fault. Just like it's not your fault that Austin got hurt. It's horrible, and it's okay to cry and show how hurt you are. But never let it define you or turn you into something bad. Austin loves you like Therese loved me. Don't shut out people who can help you get through this."

I let her pull me into a hug. It feels good when every part of me is shaking. It's getting darker out. The sun comes out just a little before it starts to set. Austin wakes up to see it one more time. I can see in his eyes. He knows he's not going to be here to see it tomorrow.

Chapter 11
Robert

I walk the pavements next to the soccer field. I'm good at soccer. It's one of the only things I'm good at but, because I'm bad at school, Dad doesn't let me play. Not until I can catch up with the year I'm behind.

There's a game going on. I hear screams and cheers for the teams. I'd want those cheers to be for me, but nobody will ever cheer for me. If only I weren't so freakin' stupid, I wouldn't still be stuck in first grade. I begged Dad not to hold me back. The teachers said I might be able to catch up, but I'm never good enough for him and so I'm stuck with little kids.

I keep walking, and I'm at the playground. It's empty and quiet. The wind moves the swings and makes them creak. This was where Austin had his party. I can't believe he actually invited me. I probably shouldn't have gone. He's a wimp, and maybe he wouldn't have told the teacher if I didn't pick on him there. Then I wouldn't have taken his scissors. Why did I do that? And how did they go into his side? He wasn't supposed to get hurt. I never wanted him dead. He's just a kid. So am I.

I sit down on the swing and move my legs back

and forth. It's almost dark out. I can't get Austin's face out of my head. He looked sad and shocked that I actually hurt him like that, but it was worse than that. He just looked so scared about dying. I stabbed him. Of course he was scared. He was bleeding so much, and I know it hurt. He probably thought he was gonna die right there. Nobody will tell me how he's doing. Maybe he already died.

I hear the Church bells down the street. Why are they ringing this late? Mass is over by now. Austin was a good Church boy. He went to Mass every week. Thinking of him brings the pictures of his blood on me back into my head.

I hold my head and scream. Make them go away. Is this God trying to punish me? I jump off the swing and run down the street to the Church. It's still crowded.

More than even on Christmas.

I don't know if there's a God. When my mom left, God didn't seem to care. When Dad made me start school a year late, and then held me back a year, God didn't care.

Maybe he agreed with Dad that I was lazy and needed more time to get real about school. But then again, Dad doesn't believe in God either. No heaven. No hell. Just darkness. I don't know why he sends me to Catholic school. Maybe because of Grandma, or because he thinks it's harder. Ms. Wells says my grades are good enough to go to second grade in the fall, but Dad thinks I should be able to make up for lost time and skip a grade, and I'm a failure until I do that. At least Austin's mom loves him, and doesn't need him to be super smart for her to love him.

I walk up the Church steps. I've never been here on my own before.

Just about every seat is taken in Church. The organ is playing a song I don't recognize.

There's one empty seat in the back pew. I sit down in it next to an old lady who is crying. She must know about Austin.

There's a stained glass of The Last Supper next to us.

Father Doyle comes out to address the crowd and thank them for coming to the prayer service for Austin Palmer. Is that what this is for? Oh no. If anybody sees me, they'll kill me for sure because I know everyone knows I'm the one who stabbed him.

I want to run out the doors, but that might make me stand out even more. Plus, I want to pray for Austin. I really didn't mean to stab him. If he dies, that makes me a murderer. He'll be dead forever, and I'll be the one who killed him.

Father Doyle wipes aside a tear. "The Palmers have been a valued family of our congregation for many years now. They're our friends, our neighbors. We stood by her side a few years ago when we lost John in an accident. We comforted Rose and the boys. We watched them grow from little babies . . . Now they need our strength and our prayers again."

Yeah, because of me. Austin's gonna die because of me. I feel tears on my cheeks, but everybody is crying. They don't see me yet.

Father Doyle walks down the center aisle. "As I'm sure you know, Austin was involved in an incident at school this week. He was seriously injured, and his condition has gotten progressively worse these past few days . . . the doctors don't expect him to survive the night."

Everyone in the Church lets out an audible and depressed sigh. Some sob louder.

I knew it. I hoped maybe the doctors could save him, and he'd get better. Then maybe everyone wouldn't hate me so much. But if he's really dying for real, then I'm doomed.

Everything gets really quiet really fast, except for the cries. Even Father Doyle is crying.

"I went to see him earlier today. I gave him his sacraments for the first time . . . for the last time. When I left him, he seemed to be in really good spirits. He was a little scared, but that's understandable. He knows what's happening to him, yet he doesn't know exactly what lies beyond this mortal place. We all know what we are told, what we believe, but there's still so much uncertainty and it can frighten any of us, let alone a child. Losing him is a loss for all of us. He would've been a strong piece of our future, but he will instead go sooner to Christ's eternity."

I make eye contact with him, and he's looking right

at me. Does he know? Is he going to say anything?

He clears his throat. "I wanted us as a community to do something for Austin. That's why you're all here, I presume. But I didn't just want us to do a service here. Not that there's anything wrong with praying in God's house, but I wanted to bring our prayers closer to the Palmers. I'd like it if we could organize a prayer vigil of sorts outside Austin's hospital room. It overlooks a grassy part of the hospital grounds, so there'd be ample room for us. I've gathered candles that we will distribute on your way out, if you'd like to participate. It'll have to be right away. Please do spread the word however you can on such short notice. If we're going to lose Austin, let's let him know how much we love him while he's still with us. Prayer is such a powerful act, and even if we don't get a physical healing, we know its results reach far beyond our heartbeats."

The Church empties out quickly after that. Everyone grabs their candles and is off to pray for Austin.

I'm almost alone in the Church now. I look up at the crucifix that hangs above the altar. I know it's just a statue, but I feel like it's really God staring down at me from heaven. Just like the soldiers killed Jesus, I killed Austin. I say it to myself again. "I killed Austin." Sure, he's not dead yet, but he will be and it's my fault. God must hate me now because Austin loved everyone. And I stabbed him.

I run out the back to the lobby. There are pictures

on a table from the carnival we had last week. The pictures show Ms. Wells making funnel cakes and Father Doyle on the dunking tank. I remember how much fun it was. For one night, Dad seemed proud of me. I even won a large Scooby-Doo.

Then I see a picture of Austin. He's sliding down from the funhouse and looks like he's having so much fun.

I jump back.

Austin looks so happy. I took that away from him and his family forever. Voices in my head scream "murderer" at me until I am crying again.

I bolt outside. It's windier now and just a little chilly. My hair dances a bit, and I can almost forget how much I want to be dead instead of Austin right now. I hear birds overhead and see a family of blue jays flying above. They don't know what I did. To them, this is a normal day. Everything is so normal for the rest of the world.

I want to run home, but I can't face Dad again. He'll just tell me to get over it and that Austin doesn't exist anymore, so I shouldn't feel guilty.

I sit on the Church steps and try to replay those moments in my head to see what I could've done to stop it. Everything. It was all my fault. If I'd just left him alone . . .

"Hello, Robert."

A jolt in my heart.

Father Doyle sits next to me. "You're in Austin's

class, right?"

Do I answer? If I lie, he'll know. If I run, he'll know. "Yes," I say. "I sit next to him." Just for one day. Not a lie.

"We're having a prayer vigil for him. Would you like to come?"

"I don't have a ride." I gulp. "My dad won't take me."

"Why don't you come with me? I'll give you a ride."

My heart pounds in my chest, and I don't know if I should go with him or run away and let him know I'm evil and should burn in hell forever for killing Austin. I don't even remember saying "yes," but I must've nodded because I'm walking to his car and taking a seat next to him.

We don't talk during the drive. We exchange a few looks, and I'm afraid he's going to ask me something. But he just sits there driving. Maybe he wants me to just confess. That's his job, I guess. To hear confessions. Maybe I should. He can't tell anybody. But I know I can't be forgiven unless I go to the cops. But they'll throw me in jail, and I'll get stabbed like Austin. But maybe that's what should happen. It's what I get for killing Austin.

As we get out of the car, Father Doyle looks me in the eye. "I'm here whenever you need to talk, Robert. It might make you feel better."

"Yeah, whatever." I take a few steps.

Then my legs give out and I'm in his arms crying.

Chapter 12
Austin

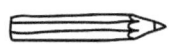

What will dying feel like? I keep asking Jesus that as it gets later and I feel like I can move less. Will it hurt like getting stabbed, or will it just be like falling asleep? Will I hear the machine go crazy, or will I not know anything? It's scary that nobody can come with me, but Jesus is waiting on the other side. And I know He will make sure I get there.

Opening my eyes hurts, but I want to see Mommy and Conner while I'm not dead. I think they know I must be dying soon because they're crying even more, and their eyes look at me like I will disappear any minute.

Conner lies beside me again and hugs me. "When you see Dad, can you tell him I miss him?"

I nod yes. I try to say anything, but my voice doesn't work much.

He says he's sorry again. I don't know why he's sorry. He didn't kill me, and he can't always be there to save me.

I'm still cold, but my body is all sweaty and sticky. It must be the evil germs inside my stab that are killing me. Mom and Ms. Wells were right. Germs are really bad.

Dr. North comes in and listens to my heart and breathing and checks all the machines.

Mommy looks at him and he nods.

Dr. North gets her out of the chair. "We don't need to keep him connected to anything . . . it won't do any good anymore. He needs to be held right now, not tied to machines."

Mommy smiles and cries and hugs him. "Thank you for everything, Doctor."

Dr. North is crying too. "I wish I could've done more for you."

He walks over to me and takes the needle out of my arm and the weird glowing thing off my finger. He even unhooks the tubes that take out my pee, and so I'm all free now.

Mommy scoops me up in her arms and kisses me and hugs me close. "Oh, Austin . . ." She cries onto me. I try to hug her and make her feel better, but my arms still can't move. My voice feels like it works a little now, but comes out as a whisper. "Love you, Mommy."

Conner walks to us and holds out his hand. "I want to hold him too."

"Conner . . ." I try to wave him over.

He gets his face close to mine. "Yeah?"

"When I die, can you still ask Mommy for a parrot?"

Conner's eyes get wetter. "That'd be mean. We get your parrot after you're dead."

"It'll make you feel better. It's okay."

Conner looks away. "Sure. I'll beg her until she listens. But you know Mom, she never listens." He sticks his tongue out at Mommy and cry-laughs like she does.

Dr. North asks Mommy if she needs anything. Mommy says no.

Mommy cuddles me close. "When you see Jesus, maybe you can pray for all of us down here who are sad. Jesus loves when his little children pray."

"I will, Mommy." I don't know if my voice says this, or if I just want to say it. But I think Mommy hears it anyway.

Nurse Judy comes in. "Have you looked out the window?"

Mommy looks at her confused. "Out the window?"

"You should see."

Mommy puts me on the bed a second and walks to the window. She gasps and takes a step back. "What is this?"

Nurse Judy touches her shoulder. "I spoke to them. They're here for you . . . for Austin."

Mommy cries more and touches her heart. "They all came for him? But why? What did we do?"

"They love you. They love him. They want you all to know that you're not alone in this."

Mommy comes over to me and picks me up again. She carries me to the window, and Conner comes too.

Outside I see so many flickering orange lights. Like a million of them! They're candles. People are holding them and rosaries. Father Doyle is at the front of them.

Robert is next to him trying not to look at anybody. He doesn't have a rosary but seems to be praying with them on his fingers. Is he here to pray for me too? Maybe he's sorry he killed me. If he's sorry, I don't want to be mad at him. I forgive him. Maybe he's finally my friend too.

"Wow . . . there's so many people," Conner says.

He's right. They each have a light, and they almost become one big light.

"Do you see them, Austin?" Mommy holds me close. "All of these people are here for you. Each light is a prayer for you going up to heaven."

"They're all for me? But why? I'm going to die."

"They're praying anyway. Even if you go up to heaven, they pray you get there quickly, that Mommy and Conner are okay. Praying never hurts. God will use it for something, and they're just letting you know that they love you and are thinking about you."

"Why? What did I do?"

"You were you. You were Austin Palmer, a beautiful, excitable, playful, happy little boy. When Jesus said that He wanted the little children to come to Him, He was talking about kids like you. You're a good boy, Austin. You're my little boy. You and Conner mean the world to me, and I think everyone in our little community knows how special you both are. We're a big family, and we need them, so they're here."

It's so amazing. They're here for me. All of these people I don't even know. Even Robert is here to pray for me. It's the most wonderful thing I've ever seen in my whole life.

My breath starts not coming out good again, and I feel so sleepy, but I don't want to look away.

Mommy picks up my hand and waves it to the people. I hope they can see me. "Tell them thank you," I say.

Mommy nods and a tear falls off her cheek and hits my nose. She kisses me and pats my hair.

We all go back to the bed and lay down on it. Mommy and Conner both hold me tight. I feel my insides trying to stop, but I keep telling them to keep working so I can stay with Mommy and Conner longer.

Conner turns my head. "You're trying so hard, aren't you? To stay. But you don't have to fight back anymore. I know I told you to fight back, but you can stop. Don't hurt anymore, Austin. Go be with Daddy and Jesus."

I look to Mommy. Her eyes say she doesn't want to say yes, but she nods. "If it hurts too much, honey . . . I don't want you to hurt anymore."

I look up and wonder what I should do. I don't know how to stop fighting my own insides. "Can you sing to me? Or tell me a story?"

Mommy sings me my lullaby. Conner tries to sing along, but his cries choke his words.

Francesco

It's my favorite song ever, but I hear another one in my ears getting louder. It's like the choir at Church, only prettier. Like a thousand million angels!

I try to breathe out, but my breath is stuck again. And this time it's not getting unstuck. I feel a weird turning inside of all of me, like I'm a balloon and all the air is let out. "Love . . ." I can't say anything else, but I hope Mommy and Conner know.

I close my eyes and listen to the angel song and try not to focus on not breathing.

I stop trying to, and maybe that's what Conner meant by not fighting anymore. I feel every part of me go all floppy and light.

One second I'm in me, and the next, I slip out of me like Jell-O. Did I die just like that? I thought it would be really hard.

A man picks me up who looks like Jesus from every picture I ever saw, only brighter and a bigger smile. He holds me and tells me He loves me.

Then I see Daddy and I smile. I missed him so much, and now we're together forever. And ever and ever.

Chapter 13
Conner

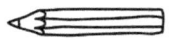

I was ready for the loud beeping and the screeching heart monitor. I wasn't ready to just feel him die in my arms like that. It was just a moment. One moment I felt Austin, and then it was like God turned him off, and everything just stopped. He was just so empty.

I kiss his cheek and look at his face. His eyes are closed like he's asleep, and his mouth is drooping open like when he's asleep. But I think it was him trying to breathe that made his mouth open. I heard him struggling, and it must've been so scary to not be able to breathe until you die.

Dr. North comes over and feels Austin's neck. He says the time it is. It's almost ten o'clock.

I thought Mommy and I would be crying harder, but maybe we don't have any more tears left.

Dr. North touches us. "You can have all the time you need, but we should be taking him soon . . . you'll be allowed to visit him."

They want to take Austin away to that place he didn't want to go to. Where they take off your clothes and put you in a drawer. We see it on TV, and we always joked that it was so creepy and weird. He's supposed to be sleeping in our bed right now. But now he's dead. Dead. I say the word in my head again. I can't think of Austin as dead. Not alive. He's my baby brother.

I hear them in the hall talk about "remains" and "the body." He's not remains. He's not just a dead body. He's Austin. Stop talking about him like he's not my brother.

All the voices get louder and more jumbled. "7-year-old male." "Stab wound." That long word that killed Austin. I don't know why they're all talking about him, but it's all so jumbled.

Mom lifts me off Austin, and I see him alone in the bed. His head is turned to the side. He doesn't just look asleep anymore. Something about him from this far away really looks dead . . . and I know it's real. He's never coming back to life. Never ever. I don't have a little brother anymore. I'm an only child. Why did God take Austin away?

Dr. North pulls the covers over Austin's head and wheels the bed away. The room feels so empty now. Just a few days ago Austin was 7 and annoying and my brother. And now he's dead, and I'm alone. It's not fair.

Mom hugs me closer and says it's okay.

She carries me out to the elevators. Ms. Wells is in the waiting room. "He's gone," she says.

Ms. Wells hugs us. We all go down together.

"You can both stay with me tonight. You shouldn't

go to the house yet. Not tonight."

"Thank you," Mom says.

We go outside, and everyone with the candles sees us.

Father Doyle comes up to us. We don't say anything. Mom just nods.

I tap her to put me down, and I walk to Father Doyle and hug him. I worry he's going to say something to me about Austin being happier now, but he doesn't. He just hugs me and pats my back.

We look at all the people. The candles are still flickering prayers, even though Austin's dead now.

Mommy walks up to them. "Thank you all. You don't know how much this means . . . how much it meant to Austin. One of the last things he got to see was everyone in this community gathering together to pray for him. That made him so happy. Because of you, my little boy went home happy. He wasn't scared, and he had more than just the love of his immediate family. He had everybody there with him. I can't ever thank you enough for giving him that. Forever, that is your gift to Austin."

Ms. Wells takes Mom aside to cry some more. I think everybody is going to leave, until they don't. They stay praying, even for an hour or two. They bring candles for me and Mom and Ms. Wells. We all pray. The rosary and other prayers. For Austin, for everyone in the hospital, for all the sick and hurt kids in the world.

Then I see Robert. And he sees me.

All my tears go away, and I feel a burning in my stomach. Is this what hate feels like? I just want to yell at him and hurt him and make him pay for killing my brother. But I stay still because nobody will let me hurt him here. But I'll get him. I'll make sure he pays for hurting Austin. Just not tonight. Tonight is about praying for Austin.

I see the guy Patrick from earlier. He has a candle too. He comes up to me and kneels down so we're at eye level. He throws his arms around me and hugs me. I hug him back. I don't know why, but I feel safe for a minute. When I look in his eyes, I see that he understands. I wait for him to say something, but he stays quiet. He pats my head and leads me into the crowd. He must know what it's like because he's good at making me feel just a little bit better.

We stay until after midnight before Ms. Wells decides to take us to her home. But even as we drive off, I see the flickering candles in the distance. I think they're going to stay there praying all night. At least Austin still has them there just outside so he's not totally alone.

Chapter 14
Robert

The vigil is still going when I walk home. It's dark once I get back. I've never been out this late before, but I can't be scared when Austin's dead because of me. I can't believe he's really dead. For real. I remember feeling his heartbeat when I sat on him at his birthday and made him feel bad. He was alive then, and I made that stop.

I go for the doorknob to the house. Maybe this will all be a bad dream, and I'll wake up and Austin won't be dead. And I can say sorry and not tease him anymore.

I see Dad sitting in his chair staring right at me. I thought he went to bed, but I should've known better.

Dad gets up from his chair and walks over to me, but I can't look at him. I already feel his eyes shooting into my skull with that look that I am not good enough.

"Robert, I shouldn't have to explain to you how a curfew works." I kick my feet together, trying to pretend like I don't.

He grabs me by my shirt. "Do not disobey me. You're a smart kid. You should be a grade ahead by now, not two behind. You will never get ahead if you keep pulling stunts like this."

"It's not a stunt," I say. "Austin died tonight . . . I had to be there."

Dad turns my face up. "I know where you were. I had someone look for you."

"Why didn't you get me then?"

"I let you have your little soapbox for one night. I know you're feeling bad about what happened, and I don't want to trivialize it. A classmate died, and I am not unreasonable. But he's dead now. He doesn't exist anymore. So you've had your cry. It's time to move on and reapply yourself. Your grades are good enough to step up. I've arranged for you to do classes over the summer. If you work at it, I can have you caught up on everything by next year. With Austin gone, you can focus on your studies instead of him. You won't have to be behind anymore."

"Who cares anymore? Dad, I killed somebody. I killed another kid. Doesn't that make you mad?"

Dad sits down in his chair. "Come here." He calls me over and sits me on his lap. "Did you mean to kill him?"

I shake my head as tears roll down my cheeks. "I was just trying to screw with him again. Like I always do. He was fun to tease. I didn't think he'd ever get hurt."

"Then you didn't kill him. It was an accident. Yes, it's sad he died. If it'll make you drop this, I'll cut a nice check to his family. But really, you need to move on. Crying isn't going to bring him back, and it's not going to advance your studies. Use this as a learning opportunity as to why you need to stay focused on your studies."

I lean my head on his chest. As scary as he is sometimes, hearing his heartbeat in my ear always makes me feel less scared. "What about the cops?"

"They came by today. We had a talk. I told them I picked you up from school, and that you came out crying because you saw your friend fall on his scissors. You tried to help him. The boy is dead. He can't testify to the contrary, and even if he could, kids lie. They tell stories. I told them I picked you up. I gave them incentive to stop asking questions. They will rule this entire thing a very tragic accident."

"But that's a lie. I did stab him. You didn't pick me up."

Dad strokes my hair. "Your entire life is over if you spend even a few years in juvie. I'm not going to let a guilty conscience make you throw your life away. I'm sorry about this Austin kid. I'm sure he didn't deserve to die like that. But he did. He's going to be a pile of bones in a few months. He doesn't have a future. You do. Nobody saw what happened. Nobody can touch you. I will make sure of that."

"I can't just pretend I didn't kill him." I grab a fistful of his shirt. "Dad, I can't sleep. I can't do anything."

Dad sets me on my feet. "It's late. You're just tired. Get to bed." He kisses me and pats me on the head.

"You'll feel better in a few days."

"Yes, sir." I pocket my hands and turn to go to my room.

Dad turns me by my shoulder and kneels to eye level with me. "Look, I know you think I'm some unfairly strict disciplinarian. Heck, I agree. I am. But I do what I do because I love you. Sometimes loving somebody means being tough on them. My dad didn't care about my grades. And I struggled in school for years. It wasn't until a teacher took the time to hold me to a higher standard that I was able to excel, and it's because of being strict on myself that I became as successful as I am. You're my son. I know you. You are not a murderer. What happened was an accident. Just because I'm strict doesn't mean I am going to stand by and let my son go down for an accident. Now, where's that smile I love?" He gently presses on my chin with his finger.

I force a smile so he'll feel better. Fighting with him isn't going to make me feel any better.

"That's my boy." He claps me on the back. "Now get some sleep."

Dad goes to bed, and I stand in the living room a moment. My stomach twists and turns, and I feel my insides yelling at me.

I rush to my bedroom and change into my nightclothes quickly. I look in the mirror. I look so pale, but Austin's paler now. I think of where he is right now. The morgue. I wonder if he's cold or if he knows that he's dead. Is he sad? I was always scared that when you die, you're stuck inside your body forever, and you know where you are and can't do anything. I hope that's not true because I don't want Austin to be stuck in a box because of me. Maybe if he doesn't exist anymore, at least he's not scared.

Standing in my underclothes, it feels drafty and almost cold. That's weird because it's so hot out. It shouldn't be cold at all.

"Why did you kill me?" Austin's voice.

I turn around but don't see anything. Must be just in my head.

"I'm sorry, Robert. I didn't mean to tell on you."

I squeeze my ears shut and jump onto my bed, burying my head in my pillow.

Make it stop. I can't hear this anymore.

I feel something on my shoulder and jump up.

I turn around to see him standing on my bed, with his usual crying eyes that I always make fun of. Only he has the hole in his side with blood dripping down.

I scream. I hope Dad doesn't hear me.

"Why did you kill me?" He holds his side. "I didn't want to die. I'm 7. I was supposed to just be 7."

"I'm sorry," I say. I jump up and grab him by the shoulders. He doesn't see me. "It was an accident. Oh, God, Austin. You weren't supposed to end up dead."

His face starts peeling off until there's just a skull there.

I scream and fall back. I bang my head on the

headboard of my bed, but I don't care. The throbbing lets me not think about Austin for ten seconds.

Then the pain stops, and he's back.

Austin's entire body becomes bones and crumples into dust. "I'm so cold." I still hear his voice. Why do I still hear his voice? "I'm sorry, Robert."

"Why is he sorry? I'm the one who killed him. I'm the one who's sorry. I'm so sorry, Austin."

He's gone forever because of me.

I remember the first day of school this year when they called Austin's name. He was so dweeby the way he walked to our group and acted all happy to be in school. When I learned he was Conner's brother, I knew he'd be fun to pick on. And he was. Why couldn't he just give up fighting back? Then none of this would've happened. Kids aren't supposed to die.

I try to close my eyes and sleep, but it's just like last night only worse. Instead of just being hurt, now he's dead. Forever. I keep seeing him lying on that floor and all that sticky, red blood all over me. He was so small, but he had so much blood inside him. We had to throw out my uniform, it had so much on it. They probably will have to throw out Austin's uniform too. Not that he needs them anymore. He's never coming back to school.

School . . . when I go back, his desk is going to be empty. Everyone's going to know I did it, and they're going to stare at me and call me a murderer. No matter what I do, I'm always going to be the reason that Austin is dead.

I turn on my side and see his bones next to me again. And his voice returns. I cry and cry until it's morning. I don't know if I am sleeping or awake all night. Maybe it doesn't matter anymore.

Chapter 15
Conner

For the first time in seven years, I wake up an only child. The morning is gray and sad, but it's not raining. Ms. Wells drives us out of town to go to Mass so nobody knows who we are. Mom isn't ready to hear how sorry everyone is. Then we go home, and the whole day passes without anybody saying anything. No calls. No talks. We don't even cry. We just sit in quiet and only eat a little bit. Then we go to bed again.

Monday morning comes, and it's still cloudy. I walk into Ms. Wells' living room. Mom isn't sleeping on the couch anymore. She's already up and staring into her coffee at the kitchen table.

"Morning, Conner," she says without feeling. "You should have . . . something. I don't want to put Ms. Wells out any more than I have, but you should eat . . ."

I grab a box of cereal from on top of the fridge and pour it into a bowl. "This is fine."

Mom looks over at me. "I'm going to go to the funeral home today to make plans. Ms. Wells said she'd watch you."

"I want to come."

"Conner, this isn't the place for kids."

"Austin's a kid. I'm his brother. I want to come."

"You'll be bored."

"Mom, he's my brother."

Mom pushes her coffee away. "Fine. You can come, but don't wander off or say anything."

I stare down into my cereal bowl a moment. "I want to see him today."

Mom looks away. "I don't think that's a good idea."

"I promised him I'd see him. I need to see him, Mom. I just do, okay?"

"You're not supposed to see . . . he's dead, Conner. He's not going to look like . . . you're just a kid. You're not supposed to see adult things like that."

I push my bowl away and get up from the table. "Austin's not supposed to be dead. How things are supposed to be doesn't matter anymore."

Mom grabs my arm. "Okay. We'll go."

I break away from her grip. "I'm not a baby. I don't need you to hold my hand like with Dad."

"There's no shame in needing someone to hold your hand, Conner. You think I'm going to be able to go make plans to bury my little boy on my own? If you have somebody to hold your hand, you hold onto them and you never let go."

Everyone who holds my hand winds up dead. Maybe it's just safer for everyone if people just leave me alone.

We drive by this funeral home almost every day. Everything is so fancy and shiny. They must want us to forget that someone is dead.

Father Doyle stands by the entrance. "I figured you could use someone in your corner."

Mom wipes her eyes. "I appreciate it, but you don't have to."

"I work with these guys every week. I'll make sure you get a fair deal."

"Fair deal . . . it's my son. I'm not looking for bargains."

"I know your financial situation is tight. Let me help."

"Do you usually negotiate with the funeral home for your parishioners?"

"Rose . . ." He touches Mom's shoulder. "We're all here for you."

She nods and we go inside. Chandeliers and fancy chairs are everywhere.

A fat guy in a suit walks up and shakes each of our hands. "So sorry for your loss, Mrs. Palmer. I heard about it on the news, and it just breaks my heart. I'm so humbled that you've chosen our funeral home to help you through this difficult time. Now if you'll follow me, we can discuss options for how we can assist you."

Father Doyle clears his throat. "Look, Ms. Palmer is on limited finances. We're looking to keep things simple."

"With all due respect, Father, I think Ms. Palmer is capable of deciding these things for herself."

Father Doyle sighs. "I know this is your livelihood. I'm not trying to judge. But she just lost her son. There's nothing she wouldn't give him, but she has to be realistic about paying for this. We both know as respectful as this establishment is, you're not just doing this out of the kindness of your heart."

Fat Guy takes a step back. "If it's a matter of paying, we have several financing options."

Mom steps between them. "Can we not treat my son like he's a used car?"

Fat Guy's mouth droops. "Of course. Why don't we talk somewhere more private?" Fat Guy takes us to an office, and Mom and Father Doyle sit in front of his desk. I sit on a couch to the side.

While Fat Guy is getting papers in the back, Father Doyle whispers to Mom, "I know even small packages will be a difficulty. I took up a collection to help you yesterday. The response was overwhelming, but these places can eat it up so easily. I want you and Conner to have enough left over to get through."

"Nobody had to do anything." She holds herself. "They did too much last time . . . but thank you."

Fat Guy returns and takes his seat. "Well, I grouped together our common services. Embalming, body washing, coffin, wake services, hearse . . . we also have a business relationship with the cemetery you'll be using, so we can streamline the payments for the tombstone, grave, and burial services and keep things very simple." He slides a sheet over to Mom. "I think this is a fair and reasonable price."

Mom cries harder. "I can't . . . this is even more than my husband's cost just a few years ago."

"Well . . . times are difficult." He swallows hard. "Costs go up."

Father Doyle scans over the sheet. "If Rose wishes, we'll be having the viewing at the Church before the service, should she choose to have a viewing at all. There won't be a need to have that here. That should help reduce this."

"Okay . . ." He writes down some numbers on the sheet. "Well, this is what I can do without that."

Mom stares at the sheet. "You're making me choose between feeding my living son and burying my dead one."

"Well, there are many things we must do for funerals. We must embalm the body and house it overnight and escort it to the Church and cemetery."

"We have a plot already . . . my husband and I bought four before he died. Just in case . . . we didn't want to be separated."

"Okay . . . well then." He scribbles more numbers.

Mom looks at them and cries. She turns to Father Doyle. "He's my baby, but I don't know if I can . . ."

He holds her. "Remember, we have what I collected."

"I can't just take money to bury my little boy. I'm

his mother. I'm supposed to be taking care of him."

I can't take hearing Mom cry. I jump up. "Stop trying to make extra money on my brother dying. He's dead, and you're trying to make us buy flowers that he can't even see."

"Conner." Mom steps up.

Fat Guy is speechless. "Well . . . why don't we go look at caskets, and maybe then we can get a better idea of cost?"

Fat Guy leads us to a room in the back where there are tons of caskets set out like cars at a car store. Most of them are for grown ups.

My stomach knots at looking at some of these. The wooden ones shine but look so tight. I'm going to be in one of these one day until it and me are dust. I run my fingers across the smooth surface and follow Fat Guy down to a corner where they have small caskets. For kids.

One of them is small and wooden like the others. I don't even think Austin will fit in one of these, even if it is nice looking.

One next to it is white and has Catholic symbols on it. It's tight and small just like the other. How are they going to squeeze Austin into that?

Both of them are over five thousand bucks.

Mom reads the labels and falls to her knees. "My baby . . ." Father Doyle holds her and eases her to her feet.

Fat Guy clears his throat. "Well, if price is an

absolute concern, our most affordable option would be this." He points to a wooden box that looks like they just made it from the trees outside. Do people actually want to be buried in that?

Mom cries harder. "I can't put my baby in that."

"Why don't we all take a break? I know this can be a very overwhelming time. Maybe a few minutes to pause will help?" He clicks his pen and leads us to the lobby.

"You can't put my brother in a box," I say.

"I'm not. It's all just so much . . ." Mom holds her head.

Father Doyle pats her shoulder. "Remember, you're not going to have to do this all alone."

"How can I pinch pennies with my son? I can't just drop him in a box and leave it at that."

He shakes his head. "You shouldn't have to choose between giving him a dignified burial and paying your bills."

"So what do I do? Even with the money you collected, this is all so much."

Fat Guy comes over again with his phone in hand. "We just had a call come in. Apparently, an anonymous donation has been made for Austin's services. It's sizeable. It will cover all or most of even our most elaborate services."

Mom stands with her mouth open. "Who would do that?"

Father Doyle takes her hand. "People love Austin

in this town. They're here for you."

Fat Guy throws on a half smile and wipes his glasses. "Well, with that in mind, would you like to return to select a casket?"

"The white one." Mom looks down. "I can't look at those anymore. I can't walk through a line of boxes for my little boy like I'm picking out furniture. That one was pretty . . . just go with that one."

"Okay." He smiles. "Then we can discuss the other matters."

She shakes her head. "I can't do this." She turns to Father Doyle. "Just go with him and pick what you think is good. I trust you."

Mom grabs my hand, and we walk out the front door.

"Why didn't we stay and pick everything else out for Austin?"

Mom doesn't say anything. We get in the car and she just sits there, head against the steering wheel, crying.

I look back at the funeral home and think about the room of caskets and the one we're gonna put Austin in. Then I think about them taking Austin here so they can drain all his blood so he won't stink when everyone walks by to look at him dead. And then I think of the shower the night of his birthday and how playful he was and how I didn't want to play with him. Then hugging him to sleep when he had a nightmare.

Then I think of feeling him stop being alive in my arms. And then my stomach hurts more.

We're going to bury Austin on Wednesday. Tonight they'll pick him up and take him to the funeral home to take out his blood and make sure he looks less dead when we look at him. Then tomorrow we're going to bring clothes for them to dress him in so he's not naked like he is now. Mom doesn't know what he should wear. His suit from when Dad died is too small and everything else feels not right.

Mom decided she wants to help dress him. She says she has to do it. I wanted to help, but she won't let me. Austin would want me to help, but I can't fight with Mom.

Especially when she's crying.

A small diner is giving us a good deal on taking everyone to lunch after Austin's buried. It's a town or two over, but they say they know what it's like to be in our shoes, and they want to help our family out.

Father Doyle takes us to get lunch before we see Austin at the hospital morgue. It feels weird ordering a cheeseburger when Austin's lying dead somewhere. Mom doesn't eat. My stomachache isn't as bad right now, so I eat it and it's good. Then I feel bad about things tasting good when I should be sad.

Father Doyle has to leave to handle Church stuff. Ms. Wells meets us at the hospital so Mom has somebody there for her besides just me. Don't they think I'm enough? I'm trying to make Mom not sad too, but everyone seems to think we aren't enough for each other without Austin.

It's already almost 3 o'clock. Four days to the minute since Robert stabbed Austin and took my brother away. Five days ago, Austin was turning 7 at this time and was happy celebrating with me and Mom. And two days from now, he's going to be in a pretty box under dirt. And he'll never get out until Jesus comes back. It's all so easy, and yet, it doesn't make any sense. It's not fair, and I still wish that, if I closed my eyes, God could change it. And we could all be a happy family again.

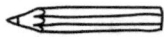

The lady who runs the morgue doesn't want to let me in. Kids aren't allowed. We're too young to see this and will get upset. Mom agrees inside, I can tell. But she promised me, and so argues our way in.

It's colder than I thought in here. I guess that's why it doesn't stink. There are so many drawers, and all of them have a dead person in them, I bet. Probably a lot of old people who died because their heart was bad. I'll bet Austin is the only kid.

She takes us to a drawer in the middle and pulls it out. I can see the shape of Austin bulging up from the sheets. His feet hang out, and there's a tag around his toe like on TV. I didn't think that part would be real.

Ms. Wells holds Mom when she asks us if we're ready. Mom says she is, and she pulls the cover off

Austin to his shoulders.

It's everything I was scared of in my head.

Mom and Ms. Wells cry and hold each other as Mom touches him. "I'll let you have some privacy." The morgue lady steps away.

"Hi, Honey," Mom says as she kisses his forehead. "It's Mommy. I'm here with Conner and Ms. Wells. We miss you so much already. We picked out a nice casket from the nice man at the funeral home. It's soft and you should . . ." She buries her head on Ms. Wells.

I walk up to him to get a better look. He's so white. His skin was always light, but there's like no color left. His eyes are still closed but look kinda flat. His mouth is still a little bit open, and I can see a bit of his teeth. One is missing from last week, with just a peek at a big kid tooth coming in, one big kid tooth grown in, and mostly baby teeth left.

His hair is pulled back. I'm not used to seeing it combed back like this. Austin's forehead looks so big and wet like this.

I think of what it must feel like to be on that metal without clothes. It must feel icky. Not that Austin feels anything right now. Why do they have to take all his clothes off? Why does being dead mean everyone who doesn't know him gets to see him naked?

I try not to cry because then Mom will send me out and say this is why kids aren't allowed in here. And I want to see Austin.

I take his hand. It's so hard and stiff. It's not soft

like his hand is supposed to be. "I'm here, Austin. I told you I'd come." I put my face close to his and try to remember what his being alive felt like. Alive and not dying. He feels so dead right now.

I look at the part of his body covered by the sheet. I feel something tugging at me, and I lift part of it up.

"What are you doing, Conner?"

"I need to see what he did to him."

I pull up the part of the cover from Austin's belly. I see the slit in his side that killed him. There's a lot of red scar around it now, but it's smaller than I thought. How could something so little kill him? Maybe because Austin was so little too.

Mom sees it too and starts crying.

Her phone falls from her purse. I don't think she sees.

Ms. Wells takes her aside and talks nice to her so she'll calm down.

I pick up Mom's phone, and then I get an idea.

I aim the phone at Austin and snap a picture. Then zoom in to his face and take another. Then another of the hole in his side. Then another of all of him. I email the pictures to the email Mom gave me for school and family, and then delete the pictures. I'll use them later.

I take Austin's hand again. "He'll be sorry, Austin. I'll make him pay." I can't stop the tears anymore. They drip onto Austin's chest.

I wrap my arms around Austin and hug him. He

feels so different than he used to, heavier and stiff. But he still feels like Austin. I tell him I still love him and step back.

Mom walks up to him and plays with his hair a minute and kisses him. We stay a bit more, and then Mom can't keep looking at him.

The morgue lady comes up and covers him again and closes him into the drawer.

Mom holds me close as we walk out. She's crying loud, but I'm holding it in so nobody thinks I can't handle it. I'll cry later. I have things to do first.

I give Mom her phone back. She pockets it without even saying anything.

With Austin's face still in my head, we go back to Ms. Wells place. Mom still can't go home yet with Austin not there.

Ms. Wells makes Mom coffee when we get in. I ask if I can check my emails to see if anybody said anything nice about Austin. They say yes.

I print out the pictures I sent. They are grainy because the room was dark, but I can see them. They'll work just fine.

I roll them up and slip them under my shirt. "Mom, can I go out for a bit to play?"

"Con . . . you should probably stay here. It's getting late."

Ms. Wells takes her hand. "Maybe it'll be good for him to get out for a bit. Help get his mind off Austin."

"Just for a little. Just to the playground. Then right

home. Okay?"

"Okay." I nod and then I go out. I feel a bit of drizzle on my face, but it's not heavy yet. So I walk.

Chapter 16
Conner

Nobody else is here at the playground. It must be the dark skies. I'm glad I'm alone. There's nobody to bother me.

I sit down on the swing and think of swinging with Austin on them a few days ago. It feels like forever. I look at the swing he was on. It creaks as the wind blows it some.

I feel the pictures under my shirt. I don't know why I brought them. I just did. Just in case. Probably was stupid. Now they're just gonna get wet.

I look up, and Robert's there at the edge of the playground. When did he show up?

Maybe it's just my head.

No, he looks too scared. He didn't think I'd be here.

"Conner." He swallows hard. "What are you doing here? It's gonna rain."

"You're here." I get up from the swings.

He kicks his feet together. "I wanted to be alone."

"So did I." I take a step toward him. "Mom's at Ms. Wells' house crying. We picked out a coffin today."

Robert's eyes water. He goes to say something, but nothing comes out. What's there to say? He killed

Austin, and he knows it.

Robert backs away from me. "You're gonna hurt me, aren't you?"

"Why would I hurt you? You didn't do anything, right?"

Robert looks down. "Look, Conner...I didn't mean to."

All my body starts shaking. I can't stop it. Without even stopping to think, I scream and charge at him and headbutt him in the stomach.

He falls back to the ground, and I jump on top of him.

"You didn't mean to do it? Is that what you wanna say?" I put my hand around his neck. "You didn't mean for him to end up dead?"

Robert starts crying. "Are you going to kill me? Is that what you want to do? Go ahead. I deserve it. That's what you want. Kill me. Make it hurt."

"I don't want to kill you."

"Liar." He tenses his lips. "I see it in your eyes. You want me to be dead like Austin is."

I pound my fist against his eye. "I don't want you dead." I can hear my voice telling Austin to fight back. "I want you alive." I see Austin trying to fight back, and then getting stabbed because of what I told him. "I want you to remember what you did."

"You don't think I remember every second?"

I take out the pictures and show him. "No, I want you to see. I want you to always have it burned into your brain what you did to my little brother." I show him the picture of Austin in the morgue. "Look. That's what he looks like right now."

Robert looks, and then tries to close his eyes and look away.

I turn his head. "What's the matter? Don't like what a dead kid looks like?"

"I didn't want him to die."

I punch him again. In the gut this time. I want him to hurt like I have since I felt Austin's heart stop. Then words spill out of my mouth. Words I heard from school and at the mall, in the movies Mom doesn't know I saw at our cousin's house. Words she says under her breath when she doesn't think I can hear. Bad, horrible, 4-letter words that taste sour on my tongue.

Robert's eyes go wide. He's scared now.

"That's right, I know all the bad words too. I didn't say them because of Austin and Mom getting me in trouble. But Austin's dead, and Mom's not here." I force his eyelids open to see Austin.

"Stop it. You're hurting me."

"Good. You should be hurt. Austin couldn't breathe much before he died, even with the oxygen." I hear the echoes of his gasps. "The infection spread all through his body until his heart stopped beating. Now he's like this." I shove the pictures in his face again. "They really do take your clothes when you die. And you go all pale and hard and cold. He's going to start to stink soon, so they'll have to take all his blood out of his body so we can bury him before he does. That's my brother now. That's what you did to him." I press the picture against his eyes. "I don't want you dead for a long time. I want you to live until you're really old so you have to go every day knowing that Austin won't ever get to grow up because of you." Because I told him to fight back. "I want you to see this picture every time you close your eyes. Like I do."

He headbutts me.

I grab my nose and fall back.

He pushes himself to his knees. "Don't you get it, Conner? I already do. Every time I close my eyes, I see him. You didn't have to see his face when it happened. I saw this horrible look in his eyes, like he knew right then that I just killed him. Oh, God, I can't get his face out of my head. So you want me to remember?" He grabs his head and screams. "I remember. I know what I did. And I'll never forget as long as I live. Are you happy? Is that what you want?"

I back away. "It's not enough. You need to see more." I take out the picture of his stab. "This is what it looked like. This is where the infection got in."

He hides his eyes and screams louder. "I'm sorry."

"If you were sorry, you'd be in jail."

Robert gets real quiet. Boom!

I fake smile. Then I wipe a tear. "See? You're so sorry until you have to get in trouble. Then you hide behind your Dad."

"Conner, I'm sorry about what I said before. I was mad. It wasn't your fault."

"Shut up!" How dare he bring that up! I pin him against the jungle gym and press my hand against his throat. "I don't care about that anymore. I care about what you did to Austin."

"I was mad." He tries to look away, but I don't let him. "He fought back and it hurt, and I wasn't thinking."

I throw him to the ground. He lands with a thud, and I wonder if Austin made as loud a sound when he hit the ground. "You can't just stab somebody by accident." I kick him in the stomach. "You just didn't care if he died. Maybe you wanted to take him away from me."

Robert shoots to his feet. He pushes me back.

I fall backward into a pile of mud. I didn't even see it start raining harder.

"I didn't want Austin to die." Robert walks to me and offers his hand to help me up.

I knock it away. "Just go away." I don't want to hear his lies or excuses anymore. I just want Austin back. "Leave me alone."

"You can't sit here in the rain."

I pick up a rock and throw it at him. Missed. "What do you care?"

His eyes are wet. I can see he knows I'm right. So he walks away, keeping his eyes on me so I don't jump him again.

I see the pictures of Austin dead getting wet and muddy. I grab them and tear them into pieces and scream.

I lie down in the mud more and let the rain fall on me and cry. For just a minute I want to lie here forever until I'm dead too so I can be with Austin again. Or at least until it doesn't hurt so much anymore.

Chapter 17
Robert

Seeing those pictures of Austin dead makes my stomach hurt more than it already did. I never saw a dead person before in my life. I always thought they'd just look like someone asleep, but he looked so different. His eyes. His face. Even his whole body just looked . . . dead. I did that to him.

The rain gets heavier now and soaks my hair dripping wet. Dad's probably waiting by the door to yell at me when I get home, but I don't care anymore.

I walk past Ms. Wells' house. I remember Conner said his mom was there. I think about him lying in the rainy mud. He must miss Austin so much if he doesn't even care about getting inside.

Before I even realize it, I'm at her door knocking. I don't remember deciding to do it, but there's no turning back now.

Ms. Wells opens the door, and I can see how shocked she is on her face. "Robert? What are you doing here?" She looks closer. "Your eye! What happened to it?"

"It doesn't matter." I pocket my hands. "I just need to talk to you or to Mrs. Palmer for a second."

"Robert, if this is about Austin . . . I appreciate the

effort, but I don't think now is the best time."

"It's about Conner."

Conner's mom is at the doorway in a second. "What about Conner? Is he hurt?"

I shake my head. "No, but he's at the playground, and it's raining . . ."

"Oh my gosh." She holds her mouth. "I didn't even think about the rain. How is it downpouring and my son is out in it, and I didn't even go get him or worry?"

Ms. Wells grabs her purse. "Our minds are in a cloud today. Let's just go get him."

Ms. Wells loads us into her car. I don't even think she thinks about who I am anymore and what I did. I see a dark red stain on the back seat. Austin's blood. I run my fingers across it.

We get to the playground, and they jump out and look around.

"Where is he?" Conner's mom stumbles around in a panic as she checks under the slide and inside the jungle gym. "I don't see him. What if he ran off and hurt himself already?"

I get out and look around. I see Conner curled in a ball under a tree. A lightning strike jolts us, followed by a huge bang of thunder.

"I see him." I point to the tree.

"He could get hurt sitting there." Conner's mom runs to the tree and tries to grab him.

Conner cries loud and throws her away. "No. I won't go. Just let me stay here. I don't want to go to sleep again. I just want to be with Austin."

She kneels down and takes his face in her hands. "Honey, I need you. I lost your brother. I can't lose you too."

"Yes you can. He was your favorite, not me."

"That's not true. I love you both more than anything. I would give almost anything to get him back, Conner. But there's one thing I wouldn't give. You. Now, why don't we talk more at home? It's not safe here."

"We were always together. You were at work all the time, and so I had to take care of him. And now he's gone because I didn't do it good. I'm the one who told him to fight back. I'm the real reason Austin's not coming home ever again."

She pulls him into a hug. "I love you, Conner. Austin loved you. You took great care of your little brother, and he knew it. He looked up to you more than anything. And I'm sorry I wasn't there enough. You needed me too, and I wasn't there."

"I had Austin. He was there, but now he's gone."

"We still have each other. And now I know I've been a little distracted these past few days. I've been so focused on how much it hurts for me that I haven't paid attention as much to you."

A loud clap of thunder. We all flinch.

"That's not true," he says. "I've been bad. I haven't been there for you. He was your little boy, and I've just cared about me being sad."

"I guess we both can help each other more from now on."

"No." He shakes his head. "I let Austin die. I told him to fight back, and he died. I should've protected him. I should've kept him safe."

Conner breaks away and tries to run. He trips and falls more in the mud.

His mom scoops him up and cuddles him close and gets mud on her. "You're safe, Conner. It's not your fault. You were the best brother Austin could ever have, and he'd be the first to tell you that if he could. Never blame yourself. No matter how much you want to. I've blamed myself so much. Maybe I could've been home a little more. But there's no good that comes from blaming yourself. We'll never have any peace if we do, and you know Austin would not want that."

Conner cuddles close to her and cries louder.

She carries him to Ms. Wells' car. "Can you drive us home? Our home?" Ms. Wells nods, and we get in the car. I sit up front next to her.

We drive to their house. Austin's house. I've never seen it before. Not even when . . . it doesn't matter now. I never thought it was so small.

Conner's mom thanks Ms. Wells and goes up to her house.

Conner hardly moves now, but his foot twitches so he must still be awake. They go inside, and the door closes behind them.

Ms. Wells turns the corner to drive me home. "Thank you for getting us. We really appreciate it."

I look out the window at the rain. "I didn't want him there alone."

"I'm proud of you."

"You're not proud of me." I turn to her, knowing she'll see my eyes wet. "You know what happened, don't you? You're going to tell the cops."

She shakes her head. "I don't know anything. If you feel that the cops should know the truth, it should come from you."

"I thought most criminals want to get away with it."

"You're not a criminal. You made a bad choice that had very real and very bad consequences. I didn't see what happened. You did. If you think what you did deserves to be told to the police, you should be the one to come forward. They can't take my word for it. Maybe if you tell them what happened, they'll be easier on you."

I swallow hard. Easier . . . I don't want easy. Austin's life is over. I could live until I'm old. How is that fair?

She turns onto my street. "I believe in the law, and sometimes, bad people need to be arrested against their will. But you didn't set out to kill him. You're just a little boy yourself. You're my student every bit as much as Austin was. I'm not going to be the one to make that decision. But if it's weighing on you so much, you have to ask yourself if you can live with the way things are now." She stops in front of my house.

"Dad's already decided for me. There's nothing I can do."

She takes my hand. "You're a good kid, Robert. Don't let guilt destroy you."

I thank her for driving me home and get out. I see Dad waiting for me by the window. I take a deep breath and go inside to get yelled at again. At least it doesn't hurt as much as seeing Austin dead. Even though I know I'll be seeing his face all night.

Chapter 18
Conner

I can't believe we haven't been home since the morning we left for school before Austin got stabbed. I'd run out the door so fast because I was mad at Mom for working late again.

It still smells of Austin. I never realized he had a smell. Not his shampoo or the stink of his farts. Just a smell of him, a feeling that he was there.

There are still all the birthday decorations in the house, reminders of when we were happy.

His toys are still on the living room floor. Not in a pile but not really away either.

Pikachu is on his back under the window, and his new helicopter is still in its box, only slightly opened for a peek. He never even got to play with it once.

"Come on, let's get you cleaned off."

Mom helps me to the bathroom. She starts a bath for me and feels the water until it's warm.

She helps me out of my clothes. They're mushy and sticky. We put them in the sink.

She disappears into her room and comes back dressed in a thin camisole and shorts. I look down and notice I'm covered in mud. It somehow even leaked through my underwear, although it's less on those parts.

I get into the tub and Mom turns on the showerhead. She tilts my head back, and the warm water rains down on me. I see black trails running down my body and into the tub water, which is all muddy and dark too.

Mom takes the soap brush and soaps me down and scrubs the mud off me. I think of when Austin scrubbed my back that night. I was so mean to him. I can almost still hear him splashing and laughing. I picture him on the other side being Austin, being his usual crazy self. If I could just go back . . .

Mom soaps my hair and scrubs the mud out. "You got yourself good and dirty, didn't you?"

I shrug. "Sorry."

Mom turns my head to her. "I love you, Conner. No matter how much either of us cry or feel pain these next few days, never lose sight of that."

I nod, and we continue washing me off until all the mud's gone.

Mom dries me off in my towel and dries my hair. I look in the mirror and it's crazy looking. I have a flash to when I was three, just before Austin was born. Mom was giving me a bath, and we ended it the same way. I had completely forgotten about getting baths alone like this. I'd only remembered having Austin there. I didn't know him then. I didn't know he'd make me even happier. I didn't know I'd lose him so soon, and it would hurt so much. I remember when Dad and Austin were alive, and we were a family. We were so happy. Now both Dad and Austin are gone, and it's just Mom and me forever now.

Mom shows me us in the mirror. "Look Conner, we're still here. You and me, we're a family. We have each other. We're going to make it through this."

I look at us. Mom looks worn and tired. I look like me still, but maybe a little older than I thought. Or maybe younger? Kind of both.

"I can't believe how big you're getting. Everyone said Austin looked like your father, and he did. But you have his features too. You have his smile."

"I do?"

She nods. "People always think you are a few years older than you are. I think it is because you carry yourself like he did. Mature, mysterious. Your face is young, but you talk and act a little older. But you know what? As mature as you are, inside you still have the heart of a child. And that heart is broken right now, and it's okay to feel. Because you're not alone, and you never will be."

She walks me into her bedroom and takes out a robe.

I hold myself shivering a moment. I'm never usually cold.

She wraps the robe around me and ties it closed. It comes down to my ankles. I remember this robe now. It was Dad's. It's not that big on me anymore like it used to look.

"Your father wore this robe a lot. I thought about getting rid of it over the years, but something told me to keep it."

I can't smell Dad on it, but for a second, it's almost like he's hugging me.

I walk to Austin's room. I see his bed still unmade. Mine's half made. It feels like last night and years ago all at the same time. I remember his nightmare.

I walk to the hamper. Our pajamas and bathing suits are still in there. I take out his Pikachu pajama shirt and press it to my chest, trying to imagine his heartbeat against it.

Mom motions for me to hand it to her and I do. She sniffs it and smiles. "I don't think I can wash this." She smiles and sets it down on his bed.

I look at the pictures of us on our shelf and the various things Austin collected to decorate our shelves. My stuff is there too, but tonight, I only see Austin's. The parrot statue grandpa bought for him when he was four. The stuffed Minion he won at the carnival at Church. Even the dinosaur puppet that is still next to his pillow.

I pick it up and slip my hand inside. "Hi, I'm Dino and Austin is my bestest friend in the whole wide world." I try to mimic the voice Austin used to do, but mine is too different, and I'm crying too much. "We should give this to him in his casket. He loved it."

Mom is quiet a moment. I think she wanted to

keep it to remember Austin, but she nods and agrees. "It was his favorite. I think he'd like that."

I open our closet and see all our nice clothes on opposite sides. We'd wear one of these to Church every week, but none of them look good enough to bury Austin in.

Then I see the crate at the bottom. It has the suit I wore for my First Communion. I slide it out and open the lid. The clothes still look as pure white as the day I wore them. "I think he should wear this," I say. "He was so excited to receive his next year . . . at least this way he'll get to wear the white suit. He's meeting Jesus now." A tear rolls down my cheek, and I wipe it away. "He should wear it."

Mom puts her arm around me. "That's really nice of you, Conner, but it might be a little too big for him."

"We can have them make it fit him, right?"

She smiles and nods. "If that's what you want."

"It is." I try to picture what Austin would've looked like going up to his First Holy Communion in this. "Everyone should see him in this."

Being in this room makes the air so heavy. Mom takes me back to hers, and we sit down on the bed. "Can I sleep in here, tonight? I don't want to sleep in our room yet. Feeling him there hurts too much."

She nods. "Yes, I understand."

We lay down together, and she pulls me close. I watch the fan blades spinning overhead and think of Austin and Dad a minute. "Do you think they can see us right now? Are they together like you and me are?"

Mom looks up. "I think so. I think your dad was waiting at the gates for Austin, and he gave him a big hug."

I say a prayer that they're both with Jesus now. And that they aren't missing us like me and Mom are missing them.

Mom hugs me closer and kisses me. "Close your eyes and try to fall asleep."

"I'm scared. I don't want to see him dying again."

"I'll be here. You don't have to be scared, Conner. Mommy's here."

I lean my head against her chest and cry. I feel her dripping tears onto my hair.

We cry together for a long time until we both dream of Austin and Dad.

Chapter 19
Robert

When I walk through the door, I get ready for Dad to yell at me again. Instead, he's in his underwear and a t-shirt on the couch, with a big bowel of popcorn, trying to juggle the TV remote.

I close the door and kick off my shoes. "Dad, what's going on?"

He smiles and pats the seat next to him. "You've been going through a lot lately. And I know I've been hard on you for what happened with Austin. You have been working hard to pull your grades up, and I have still been treating you like a slack off. That's not right. So I figured we should have a father-son night together doing something we used to love doing."

"Dad, I don't know if I should be having fun tonight."

He looks closer at me. "Is that a shiner?"

I touch it. It hurts but I deserve it. "I ran into something. I wasn't paying attention."

"What happened to Austin still got you down?"

"His family is really sad . . . of course they're sad. Austin died because of me."

Dad sighs. "Look, Robert, you know how I feel about

that. In time, I hope you'll come to see things my way. But Austin's dead and you're not. You shouldn't have to be miserable all the time. It's been so long since we really did anything together. Almost since . . ."

I look away. I don't want to think about Mom tonight. I used to be jealous of Austin and Conner because at least their dad died. That's why he wasn't there. Even if they missed him, they knew he loved them. Mom just walked out one morning because she didn't like us anymore, and then never thought about us again. Did she stop loving me? Why wouldn't she even call?

Dad gets up and puts his hands on my shoulders. "We used to hang out together so much. Watch movies, go out to eat. How about we hit up the old diner tomorrow before school?"

Memories of buttery pancakes and golden eggs fill my mind, as well as explosions and "Ahnuld." It used to be my favorite thing in the whole world, hanging out with Dad. Before he made me start school late and repeat a grade, before Mom left, before last summer.

I hear the microwave beep and smell fried chicken and mac 'n cheese. Our favorite TV dinner. Maybe it's not wrong to have fun one more night.

I throw off my shirt and pants so I'm in my underclothes like Dad. He gets the dinners and shuts the lights.

"That's my boy," he says.

The dinners are bigger than the old ones. "You're

a bigger boy, now. You're gonna be a man soon." He hands me mine and tosses me a Sprite.

Dad plays the movie. It's a new one, but it's really good. Dad doesn't try to hide the grown-up scenes from me this time. Maybe he finally thinks I'm a big boy now.

After the movie, it's almost time for bed. We gather the empty bowl of popcorn and the dinner trays and bring them to the kitchen. I shower and brush my teeth. I even use Dad's shampoo. It smells stronger, but it smells like Dad.

Dad kisses me goodnight and goes to bed too.

It was a good night. More fun than I've had in a long time. Then I think of Austin, Conner, and his mom having fun. Playing, watching movies, having a special dinner. I was feeling so happy, and now, all the sad returns and hits me in the chest. Tears spill out, but I don't want Dad to hear me. Conner will never play with Austin again. He loved him so much, and I took him away.

I roll on my side. Austin's there again. He looks just like he did in the pictures Conner showed me. It looks so real. I can almost reach out and touch him.

Then the body disappears, but I still can't stop thinking about it.

Having so much fun was great, but I can't keep being sad every time I have fun. I can't keep seeing Austin. It's not fair that I get to have fun. Maybe this will only go away if I make it right.

I get out of bed and tiptoe down the hall to the living room. I slide open Dad's desk and get a pencil and paper. I take them to my room and sit down at my desk, turning on my writing lamp.

"I hope you get it, Dad." I smooth out the paper and think of what to say. "If you want me to be responsible, I have to do this."

We get up early so we can go to our favorite diner a few towns over. Anderson Family Diner is the best. They have kids working there sometimes, but they're fast and it makes it feel like a home.

A young guy in sandals spins over to our table with a smile. "Hey, I'm Mason and I'll be taking care of you this morning. You two wanna start with some OJs?"

Dad nods and then orders a western omelet with a Belgian waffle.

Mason turns to me. "How bout you? Same as Dad, or going to go off on your own a bit?"

"I like the cheese omelet. But the waffle sounds good, so I'll get that with it."

"Then cheese omelet and a Belgian it is." He smiles and takes our menus. "I'll be right back with breakfast."

Dad watches as Mason strolls away. "He's gotten so much older since the last time we were here. You know, when he was a few years older than you are now, he used to look sad all the time, but he's happy again. See? You don't stay sad forever."

I shrug and tuck my hands under the table.

Dad leans over. "Still upset about Austin, aren't ya?"

I tense my lips. Dad didn't see my note yet. I think of telling him, but I know he'll talk me out of it. Then I'll never stop being sad. He'd never let me do this. No parent would. So he can't know. "I'm fine," I say. "This is nice. I've missed going out to eat with you. I think school will be great today with a good breakfast."

Dad smiles at me. "Now that's the attitude I like to hear from you. Keep it up, and you'll be a few grades ahead of Conner before long."

No, I won't. "Maybe." I force a smile.

"I'll take a maybe." He points at me. "Definitely starts with a maybe."

If only I could've been like this sooner, maybe I wouldn't have to do this. I would've said sorry to Austin and Conner, and even if they still hated me, everyone would be happy.

Mason brings our food. "This looks really good, guys. And I'm not just saying it because my friend made it."

Dad thanks him, and we start eating. It tastes even better than it looks.

"Your classes this summer will have a week or so break. How would you feel about going on vacation again?"

I swallow hard. Why is Dad offering all these nice things now? Is he trying to make me do better at school, or does he know what I'm going to do?

"We haven't gone on a vacation since Mom left."

"That's exactly why we need to start doing it again."

I smile. A vacation would be so much fun. I loved going to the ocean when I was little. A part of me wants to go again and just forget about . . . no, I can't go again. It's not fair. I have to do this.

"How about our favorite beach spot? We're not that far, you know. We live ten, fifteen minutes away, and we haven't been to the beach since you were five."

I shrug. "We're busy."

Dad laughs. "Okay, now you're trying too hard." He takes a bite of waffle. "You loved the ocean. You loved the beach. And you loved singing in the showers after we got off."

I giggle. "Did not."

"Did too. Dancing too. Do you know how awkward chasing a five year old singing *Journey* is?"

I blush. I remember that. I wasn't afraid of anything then. That day was the most fun I ever had.

"I have video of you building a sand castle while singing *Journey*, you know." He points his fork at me. "I'll show you tonight."

"Dad, you're embarrassing me." I eat a piece of egg. It's the best. "Stop before somebody hears. Plus, you know I can't sing."

"You're right. You can't, but you still try."

I laugh louder. I see Mason look at us and laugh too. We must look silly. I almost think about maybe waiting until tomorrow. But if I wait, I'll never stop

166

waiting.

We finish our meals, and Mason clears them away. Dad pays the bill and leaves Mason a 20 for his tip. "Dad, that's a lot."

"He's a good waiter," he says. "And the food is the best around."

As we get up to leave, I turn to Dad. "Hey, Dad, about that, could you promise me something?" We walk out.

"Sure thing, buddy. What is it?"

"You said you want to go to the ocean. But sometimes we plan things, and it doesn't happen."

Dad cracks a smile. "You're afraid I'm going to back out later, right? Not going to happen this time, Robert."

"No matter what happens, promise me you'll go. No matter what! No excuses."

"Okay!" He throws his hands up in joke defense. "No matter what, we'll go."

I throw my arms around him and hug him tight. I try not to let him see me cry.

"You sure you're okay, Robert?"

I pull back and smile. "Yeah. Let's go to school."

When I see school coming up, I turn to Dad. "I've missed spending time with you so much. This has all been so much fun. It's been the best thing in the world. Thank you. I love you, Dad."

Dad pulls back with a shocked smile. "What's going on with you, kiddo?"

I shrug. "Nothing. I should go. You're the best, Dad."

"See you later."

I tense my lips. "Yeah." I wave and close the door. I take a deep breath to calm my pounding heart, and then I walk into school.

School is too normal. A few of the kids look at me, and then look at Austin's empty desk. I feel him watching me all day. It's eerie not seeing him there. But nobody fights me. Nobody calls me a murderer. Too much is too normal. It's almost worse than being yelled at because I know what I did.

After the last bell rings, I wait for everyone to go so I can talk to Ms. Wells. I throw up in the bathroom twice before I can get up the nerve.

She walks over to his desk and opens it. His books and pencil case are left in the disorganized way he left them the day he was stabbed.

I walk up to her desk. "I'm sorry," I say. She looks up at me. "I know, Robert."

"When's the funeral?"

"Tomorrow." She wipes some tears. "If you want to come, I can have you not marked absent."

I swallow hard.

Then Conner walks in.

We lock eyes, and I prepare for him to hit me again.

Conner looks at Austin's desk and tries not to cry.

"I just wanted to see his desk again. You're going to have to empty it soon."

"Not right away. The year's almost over. We can keep it a few more weeks."

Conner turns to me. "Sorry about your eye."

I pocket my hands. "It's fine, man."

"I got something I need to say to you."

"I already know how much you hate me."

Conner shakes his head. "No, that's not what I want to say."

I look closer at him. He's crying, but he doesn't look mad. "I'm sorry."

Sorry? What does he have to be sorry for? "Conner . . . I'm the one . . ."

"I shouldn't have hit you. I shouldn't have yelled at you, or showed you those pictures. And back last year? I shouldn't have said what I did."

I feel my eyes tearing up. I almost let myself remember, but I stop before I lose my nerve. "You don't have to forgive me. I killed Austin. Nobody should ever forgive me."

"You're sorry. Hating you wouldn't make Austin happy. He only wanted you to be his friend. He didn't like people angry."

Ms. Wells touches Conner's arm. "I'm proud of you, Conner. You've really shown some maturity."

I look down a second. "That means so much, but even if you do forgive me, *I* don't forgive me. I did something so bad and Austin's . . . I can't just keep going on like nothing happened. I can't do it. I was so mean to him, and I don't even know why anymore. But now that he's dead, I need to make things right in the only way I can."

Conner stretches his hands behind his back. "I know your dad made it so you won't have to go to kid jail. It's okay, Robert."

I shake my head. "Dad doesn't know about this. I'm going to pay for what I did."

Ms. Wells leans in close. "Are you sure? Robert, this is a big decision."

Conner takes me by the shoulders. "I wanted to see you hurt so much but . . . it doesn't help. You don't have to do this, man. You don't have to go to jail."

"Do you really think that, or are you just being nice? Killing Austin needs to be punished."

Conner is quiet. I can tell he doesn't totally want me to go free. I'm doing the right thing, even if he doesn't know it yet.

Ms. Wells stands up and hugs me. "It might not be as bad as you think, Robert. It was an accident. They might go easy on you."

I shrug.

"Do you want me to go with you?"

I shake my head. "I need to do this by myself."

I take out envelopes with my letters. I give one to Ms. Wells and one to Conner. "Don't read these until later. They'll make sense. I can't ever tell you how sorry I am. But maybe these can help start. Goodbye,

Conner. Bye, Ms. Wells."

I walk out. I hear them call out to me, but I don't turn. I can't risk them stopping me.

As I walk outside, I don't feel my backpack. Doesn't matter, I guess. I don't need it anymore.

I feel tears on my face, but I wipe them aside. Almost time.

Is God real? Am I going to hell? If God is real, I hope He understands. I hope He can forgive me. Austin? If you're still up there somewhere, I'm so sorry.

I get to the intersection of the main street. It's crowded. People are everywhere, and cars are speeding by. I walk down a bit so I'm away from the traffic light.

I stand there waiting, every part of me tight. It almost hurts knowing. This must've been what Austin felt like.

I take a step into the street. I see the bus coming toward the corner.

"Robert! Stop it."

I turn to see Conner and Ms. Wells running at me. I don't have much time.

I walk further into the street.

"I forgive you, Robert. Please, don't."

For one split moment, I think that maybe he's right. Maybe it doesn't—

Chapter 20
Conner

One second, he's there, and the next he's gone. First there's a crack. It's part bang and part crunch. But it's so fast, it's gone before I can even really hear.

The bus brakes screech so loud. Everyone screams. Then I see him.

In the street.

There's blood everywhere around him. His arms and legs are splayed out, and I can see him looking back at me. Only he's not really looking at anything.

Ms. Wells and I rush over to him. She tries to hide my eyes, but I throw her away.

Everyone is gathering around, but Ms. Wells is the only one who goes up to him. She feels his neck, but I don't know why. He looks so broken, and his bones look like they got messed up. His pants are wet by his crotch. Did it hurt when it hit him, or did he die right away?

Robert's dead. Just a few feet away, another kid is dead. There's even more blood than with Austin. Is his neck twisted, or is his face just turned to the side like that because he died?

Ms. Wells cries as she holds his hand. "Why did

you do this, Robert? This wasn't what anyone wanted. This isn't what justice for Austin looks like." She kisses his hand, and it drops to the ground. She reaches down and slides his eyes closed.

The bus driver gets out and starts yelling that he didn't see the kid. He just appeared, and it was too late to stop. Some woman yells at him and says he's drunk, and he curses and says it was the kid's fault. Everybody's yelling and trying to blame somebody, but nobody seems to really care that Robert's lying there dead.

Ms. Wells runs to me, but sees the blood on her hands and pulls back. Another student's blood on her. Another dress she'll have to throw out.

"Conner, you shouldn't see this."

I can't look away. I hated him so much. He killed Austin. But seeing him like this hurts so much. He shouldn't be dead either. We used to be . . .

I run away, crying, screaming.

Ms. Wells calls for me, but I don't listen. Robert killed himself because of me, and now he's gone forever too. Kids shouldn't ever die like this. Not Robert. Not Austin. Am I going to die? Everything's spinning and it's crazy.

I stop and catch my breath a second. My hands shake as I read his letter. I imagine his voice reading each word. These were some of the last things he'll ever say. He thought he had to die to make up for killing Austin. You were wrong, Robert. You did something very bad, but you shouldn't have died too. I start running again. I don't know where, but staying still makes my chest hurt more.

I see the Church coming up. I turn and run inside. I run to the altar and ask Jesus . . . I don't even know what to ask Him anymore.

Father Doyle sees me and runs to me. "What's wrong, Conner? Did something happen?"

"It's Robert." I cry and try to talk, but my words come out all scrambled.

"Slow down." He helps me take breaths.

"I killed him. I said really mean things to him, and he walked in front of a bus. I didn't keep Austin safe, and now, I made Robert die. Oh, God, I'm so sorry. Am I going to hell now? Is Robert in hell? Did I send him there?"

I cry harder, and he hugs me tight. I tell him things I didn't even know I felt. He says I'm forgiven.

We go back to where Robert's dead. Father Doyle says a prayer over his body.

They rope off the scene and drop a sheet over him, but his hand's sticking out. "Robert!" I hear a man's voice. I look up and see him running toward us with a panicked look on his face. Must be Robert's dad. Did they call him, or was he here to pick Robert up? The cops tell him to stay back. "I have to find my son."

A policewoman with long blonde hair flashes a badge and asks him some questions. They take him to the body and pull the sheet up so he can see. He screams and tells them that's his son. He demands to know what happened, but they say they're still trying to piece it together.

He picks up Robert. The cops try to stop him, except the blonde policewoman. She seems to understand.

He asks Robert if he knew this morning. "We have to go to the ocean." He pulls Robert close to him. Robert's head and arms tilt back like they're just hanging onto the rest of him by tiny threads and not bones.

The blonde policewoman asks Ms. Wells and me a lot of questions, but I can't answer them, and they all became a blur as the day gets later. Eventually, they take Robert away. The morgue at the hospital is small. I'll bet they put Robert right next to Austin.

It's weird. They sat next to each other that last day, and now they'll keep them next to each other for one night when they're both dead. Dead. I can't believe another kid I know is dead. Right in front of me. And not because he was hurt or sick, but because he was so sad that he wanted to stop living. It doesn't make sense. Being hit by a bus must've hurt so much, even if he died very quick.

They pull away with Robert's body, and his dad is left crying in the streets. I think about going to him, but I hear my name behind me. Mom.

She runs to me and pulls me into a hug. "I heard a boy was hit by a bus and . . . I was so scared I'd lost you too. Oh, Conner, if something happened to you. I couldn't." She kisses me and hugs me tight.

Robert's dad sees and shoots us a mean look, but he walks by without saying anything to us. What can he say to us? He knows who we are and what happened to Austin.

Mom asks what happened. I tell her about Robert. How I forgave him. How he walked in front of a bus. But not about last summer. Not yet.

Ms. Wells comes over, and Mom hugs her. She's still shaking from seeing Robert get hit.

"Will you be okay?" Mom pats her back.

Ms. Wells nods. "I'll be fine. You shouldn't worry about me. You have enough to worry about."

"His clothes are in the car . . . the funeral home said they'll be picking him up later tonight." Mom paces a moment. "It's going to be hard tomorrow. Are you sure you can still handle this?"

"You're my friend. I wouldn't be anywhere else but there for you."

Mom takes me aside so we can leave. I look back at Robert's blood in the street.

How much did he have to hurt inside to hurt himself like that?

Chapter 21
Conner

We're going to bury Austin today. They already have a grave dug next to Dad's.

We drove by the cemetery, and I can see the tent from the road.

Mom dropped Austin's clothes at the funeral home last night. She wanted to dress him herself, but after a minute of it, she couldn't handle it and ran out crying. She said he looked more peaceful after they'd embalmed him. His stab was covered over, and she said he'd look really handsome in his suit.

We saw Robert's dad coming in as we were leaving. He said he was only picking out an urn for when they cremate Robert. He said something about scattering the ashes over the ocean, and that nobody would come to a funeral anyway because of what Robert did to Austin. He's wrong.

When we walk up to the Church, I have a knot in my stomach. We're only going to see Austin one more time, and then we'll never see him again. But it'll be a long see, as we'll have to stand next to him dead for an hour while people I don't know come and cry and say things to make us not feel so sad.

Father Doyle meets us at the door. "They just brought him here." There's a huge flower display on the altar. It was a gift from somebody.

The small white coffin is being wheeled to the middle of the front of the altar. I didn't like looking at the casket at the funeral home, and knowing Austin's in there makes it even harder to look at. Even though it is very nice for Austin.

Fat Guy comes in and hugs me and Mom and asks how we're doing.

I don't say anything and walk up to the casket and run my hands along it. It's smooth and shiny. It looks good under the flowers.

Fat Guy asks if we're ready. Mom is quiet a moment, but says yes. So he opens it. It opens in two halves. And we see Austin.

My white suit is on him perfectly. He would've looked so good on his First Holy Communion. His hands are folded at his stomach, just over where the stab was, with a rosary between them. He has a flower on his chest and a crucifix pin on the white tie. The white shoes rest against the edge.

Dino and Pete are on each side and lots of pictures of Dad and us.

Austin's eyes are rounder than when I saw him in the morgue, and his mouth is closed so he looks calm. They must've done something so it doesn't open.

Austin's head is tilted a little to the side. I don't remember Dad's being that way, but it kind of fits

Austin. I wonder if his body just went like that, or if they moved him like that.

"Austin, it's Conner. I'm here." I touch his hand. It feels so cold and not like Austin. "If you see Robert up there, tell him I'm sorry. I wish none of this ever had to happen so we'd all be friends." I lean my head down against his face and kiss his forehead. They combed his hair down in bangs that Austin didn't like to wear, except for pictures. It's weird. In his white suit, he almost looks a bit older, like he would've been when he received it with the rest of the kids.

Father Doyle touches my shoulder. "He was a good boy. He looks distinguished. He may not have gotten the ceremony, but he received Our Lord with joy. It was so good of you to give him your suit."

I shrug. "It looks good on him."

Mom is quiet. She stands over Austin and whispers things in his ear I can't hear.

"His body will be in this until the end of the world?"

Father Doyle kneels down and looks me in the eye. "It seems so long, I know. But with God, a minute is an eternity, and an eternity is a minute. When you go to Jesus, it'll be like you never were apart. Pray for him. Ask him to pray for you. You don't have to just miss him. You're still brothers. Remember that."

I nod and wipe a tear away. "It just hurts. It really hurts. This is really going to happen."

He pulls me close, and I cry on his shoulder.

I look up and see Mom reaching down and hugging

him.

Austin looks good. They did a good job. Everyone will like it. I hope God lets Austin's soul see how nice his body looks.

Fat Guy sets up kneelers in front of Austin's coffin.

The Church doors open. It's Ms. Wells. First one here to see him. Father Doyle steadies Mom. "I'll be right here."

Ms. Wells and Mom hug. She hugs me too. There's nothing left we can say that we didn't say before, so we just hug tighter.

She goes to Austin and kneels down and prays. She touches him and kisses her finger and then touches his cheek.

Cousins I haven't seen since Dad died show up and tell us how sorry they are and how great Austin looks. "They did such a good job. He looks like he's just asleep. If there's anything you need, just let us know." It's like they all practiced what to say.

Dr. North and Nurse Judy come together. They say the same things, but somehow it feels like they mean it more. I'm glad that they came here for him. I don't think they do this for all their patients, but Austin is special. He would've loved that they're here.

Some kids from school come. I'm surprised their parents let them come and see one of their classmates dead. They all seem so quiet as they walk by his coffin. Their parents too. I hear them whisper that they are sorry. I'm not sure what for, but maybe this is to remind them of important things.

Patrick comes in a bit later. He walks up to me and hugs me. He doesn't say the things the others do. He knows better. He hugs Mom too. I explain who he is, and she thanks him for helping me. He kneels before Austin, and I hear him tell him that he'll ask his brother to introduce himself so he's got another friend in heaven. He goes to sit in the back, but I tug on his arm and ask him to sit up front behind Mom and me. I want somebody close by who's been here before.

When the funeral Mass is about to begin, they give Mom and me one last moment to look at Austin. This is the last time we'll ever see him until we die too. We whisper his song in his ear one more time, and then they close his coffin. And we don't see him anymore.

The Mass begins. Father Doyle wears black and explains things for the people who aren't Catholic. When I turn around, I see that the Church is full. I didn't even realize so many people were coming, or that they knew Austin. But I'm glad that they are here for him.

Father Doyle chants some things in Latin, and says that this is a Requiem Mass. I don't quite understand all that, but I know it's important.

At the end, he gets up to speak to everyone. "One of the highlights of my years at this parish has been seeing our families. We have good families in this parish. Jesus said, 'let the little children come to me, and do not hinder them, for the kingdom of heaven is made for such as these.' Austin Palmer exemplified to the max the kind of child Our Lord was referring to. Yes, ask his mom and brother, and I'm sure they'll find faults." Everyone chuckles. Father continues, "But he was a good boy. He was a loving boy. He always tried to help people, and he loved his faith. One of the highlights of his last days was getting to receive Our Lord in the Eucharist. I've never met a child more excited." He fights tears. "Because of Austin, I am a better person, a better priest. I've seen in him the purity, the childlike faith, the wonder that we all aspire to. And while I will forever lament the fact that his life was cut so needlesly short, I will forever be grateful for every minute he spent on this earth. We all learned so much from him, and I don't even think we realized it. And, as much as we all wish Austin were able to continue living among us, I ask that we keep his memory alive by keeping him in our hearts, by praying for him and for others that have gone on to their reward, and by striving to show love and kindness to all people the way Austin would. The way Christ commands us to. To Rose and Conner, I offer you not only my condolences and prayers, but also my thanks for helping to shape a fine young man with your own love. And for sharing him with this community by your participation with us. May we continue to walk with you, in this your time of need. And may your family continue to cling to the Christ that Austin so very much loved."

Silence. What can anybody else say? Father steps down and prepares to end the Mass.

I stand up and walk to the center. I need to say something for Austin. He's my brother.

"Because of Austin, I was a big brother." My chest shakes. "Because of him, I had the best friend in the whole world every day and every night. I had somebody to protect and to cheer me up. Because of Austin, I had a great life, even when things were bad. And because of Austin, I'm going to have a hole in my heart forever, but because of him, I'll make sure I make him proud every day. Because of Austin, I was a brother, and I still am. He's always going to be my little brother." I turn to his coffin and hug it. "Austin, I love you. Wait for me in heaven. Okay?"

Mom and Patrick both run to help me to my seat. I hear people crying in the pews. It's almost five minutes before Father can bring himself to finish the Mass so we can all go to the cemetery.

After everyone is in their cars, Mom and I stand alone with Austin's coffin in the Church. I almost want to open it to look at him one more time, but I know we'll never stop wanting to look one more time. We watch as they roll it into the hearse, and then we're alone in the Church with just the flowers and Jesus.

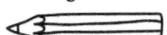

Dad's grave is under a cloth so the cemetery people can bury Austin. Fat Guy has people roll his coffin out of the hearse and over his grave.

I hear one of the cousins talking with one of the old great uncles about how the green vault in the grave is to protect the ground around the coffin and not the body.

Whatever that means. As long as Austin's grave looks nice.

Mom and I stand up front while Father Doyle prays. We pray for Austin's soul and all the souls of the faithfully departed, and he asks everyone to remember Mom and me too. Sometimes it feels like I'm stuck in my knotted body, and other times, I feel like I'm watching this whole thing from somewhere else.

We all put a rose on Austin's casket, and then everyone leaves. While other family members talk with Mom, I see them lower Austin's casket into the ground. Now it's real. Austin's buried. I knew he wouldn't be alive again, but knowing he's buried for good now makes it all hit me even harder.

I can't eat anything at the restaurant, even though the waiter named Mason is nice and tries to cheer me up. Mom can't eat either, but almost all the family members we haven't seen since Dad died can chow down pretty good. I guess they don't miss Austin like we do. Thinking of him alone in that coffin now just makes me want to throw up, but I can't because I don't want people telling me it's going to be okay anymore.

Chapter 22
Conner

I go back to the playground in the late afternoon. People come over to the house after lunch to cry with Mom. I can't stay there while everyone cries and tries to make me talk about how much it hurts to miss Austin. Mom lets me go out, as long as I promise not to roll in the mud or get hurt.

It feels good to be out of my suit, even if I was doing it for Austin. The air is thick today, even without the sun. So it feels better in shorts and a shirt.

I watch the other kids playing on the slide as I swing. I think of how Austin would probably want to play with them. He could play with anybody, but kids just ignored him after they were done. Austin wanted friends so much. Why didn't anybody want to be his friend after they were done playing? Maybe people just don't like us.

I look up and see Patrick helping a girl use the monkey bars. He sees me when he puts her down. He says something to a woman who is also helping the kids and runs to me.

"Hey." He motions to the swing. "Mind if I take a seat?" I shrug.

He sits on the swing next to me and starts swinging with me. "We have a camp starting in a week or two. There'd be lots of kids your age. Might be something you'd want to do this summer."

"I don't think so. It wouldn't be fair to Austin."

Patrick looks down and grips the swing tighter. "I was just a little younger than Austin was when my twin brother and my dad died in a car crash."

I look away.

He continues. "I had a friend a few years later who . . . died. I didn't want to do anything either. But here's the thing. The fact that they were gone didn't mean I deserved to be sad forever. You'll never stop missing him, but that doesn't mean you can't love and be friends with other people too."

"I'm sorry about your brother."

He stops his swing. "We used to come to this playground a lot. We had a lot of fun. That's why I started to volunteer at the rec center here. It let me be close to something we liked doing, close to him. And I could make some new friends. Even though most of them are busy a lot now, I still want to help the younger kids now that I'm older."

"Is that why you're trying to help me?"

He sighs. "I've seen that look on your face before. In the mirror. On my friends. And I know I can't just pep talk it away. Coming here won't erase your pain, but it could give you something good so it's not just pain anymore."

"I don't think Mom could afford camp."

He smiles and touches my swing. "Well then you can be a volunteer like me and help me out. What do you say? We don't have to talk about anything you don't want to. We'll just focus on the camp."

"I'd have to ask Mom."

"I'll ask her for you."

I look away. I went to camp last summer. It was so much fun. But that's what started all of this.

"Patrick, there's something nobody knows. Not even Mom."

He shoots me a confused look.

I hop off the swing. "Can you do something for me?"

We haven't been to the beach since Dad was alive. Austin loved it. We played in the ocean and built sand castles all day, and then Dad took us to the boardwalk at night. We had fries and pizza and ice cream. We went on rides all night, and Dad won us toys at the balloon burst and the big spinning wheels. It was the latest Mom ever let us stay up, and Austin was talking about it for weeks.

Being back here at the boardwalk alone hurts. It still looks the same. Some new places and rides, new games with new prizes, but every strip of wood reminds me of Austin. I can almost hear his laughter in the wind from the ocean.

Patrick walks beside me. "How are you going to

find him?"

I look around. There are so many people. I hope I didn't miss him. "I don't know. We might be too late. Or maybe he'll be here later. Thanks for driving me."

"You got it, bud. I just don't want you to feel disappointed if we can't find him. How do you know he's even here?"

"I can't explain it." We walk onto the pier that hangs out over the ocean. There aren't as many people here. A man holds his little boy up against the rails to see the ocean. They look like Dad and Austin.

I look over and then I see him. Robert's dad. He has a shiny container in his hands. It looks like the stuff they make coffins with, only much smaller. They must've put Robert in there after they burned him to dust.

He leans against the rail and presses the urn to his chest. He's trying not to cry, but I can see tears.

I walk up next to him and touch him.

He jumps back and looks me over, shocked. "Conner, right?" He swallows hard. "Look, if you're here to gloat . . ."

"I'm not. I'm here for you. For Robert."

He chuckles. "Why? You hated him. He killed your brother, remember? You're probably glad he's dead."

I shake my head. "I wanted to be here to see him off. This is gonna be like his funeral."

"You should go home. Your mother will need you tonight."

"He was my friend."

Robert's dad looks down at me. His eyes are shocked and wide. "You don't have to lie for my sake."

"I'm not lying." I look to Patrick, and he nods. "Robert was my friend. Or he used to be. We met last summer when we went to camp."

His face freezes, and I see a drop of sweat spill down from his gray hair and mix with a tear as it rolls onto his shirt. "I didn't want to send him. But I thought maybe clearing his head at a camp might help him refocus in the fall."

"We couldn't afford it, but we won a contest that got me in. It was just three weeks, and I know Austin missed me, but I thought it would be so much fun." I bite my lip and try not to make my voice shake. "But when I got there, I didn't know anybody. Everybody else had friends from school, but they didn't want to talk to me. Then I saw Robert sitting alone, and I went and sat down next to him. Turns out he didn't know anyone either. So we talked to each other. We started being friends, and we did everything together." I take out a picture of Robert and me from camp. We're sitting around a campfire, smiling like we'd always be friends. A camp counselor took the picture and gave a copy to both of us when we were leaving. I kept it in one of my comic books. I never even showed it to Mom or Austin. "We were never alone. We slept in the same cabin and played so many cool games. I loved having a brother, but it was great to finally have a best friend who was closer to my age and who was a friend I chose to be friends with." I hand him the picture.

He takes it and lets himself almost smile, just for a split second. "I never saw this picture . . ."

"He ripped his up." I flick away a tear. "We had a big fight." I swallow hard as I remember it. I thought we were gonna be friends forever. I couldn't wait for him to meet Austin. "The last day of camp, we got picked up, but we agreed to keep playing at the playground. The first day we did, we talked about going to school. I thought he was only a few months younger than me, so maybe we'd be in the same class. He said he was really a year younger than me. He'd lied about his age before so I'd like him, and I told him I didn't care. We were still close in age, so we'd be a year apart. He said you didn't think he was ready to start school, so you kept him behind a year. I started to laugh because it was starting to sound really weird. Then he said he didn't do grades good, so you made him stay back another year. I said that would mean he was still going to be in first grade in the fall. I laughed at him, and said he'd be the only 9 year old ever in first grade. And that he must feel really dumb to be so far behind. I even joked that he'd be an old man still in school. That made him mad. He hit me and yelled, and we started fighting and saying things, and then we weren't friends anymore. He ripped up the picture of us and threw it in the trash. When he was put in Austin's class and learned he was my brother, I think he picked on him to get back at me. If I wasn't so mean to him, none of this would've happened."

Robert's dad looks down and shakes his head. "You're kids. You say mean things sometimes."

"I'm so sorry." I cry and hug him. "I made your little boy do something that took him away from you."

He pats my head and nudges me back. "No, it's not your fault. It's mine. I'm the one who made him start late. I struggled in school, but my parents didn't care. School just kept passing me along with Ds. I eventually got my act together, but I didn't want the same for Robert." He runs his fingers down the picture. "His birthday is in a few weeks. He's supposed to be in third grade going into fourth. But I held him back a year. His mother had run out on us, and he was acting out. I didn't think he was ready. I had him do study programs to prepare him, but then in first grade his grades were all Ds. They offered to pass him along and get him help, but I insisted they hold him back. I thought being two years older than everyone in his class would shake him up. And it did. He pulled his grades up. I had planned for him to catch up over the summer through some home study courses. I could get him caught up in a year or two, even ahead of the game. I knew he was smart. Once he applied himself, he'd be brilliant."

"He seemed smart. That's why it was so funny to me. Why would he be held back?"

Robert's dad sighs. "It was all me and my stupid

standards and discipline. You didn't push him to this, Conner. I did."

"Maybe we both were mean to him." I look at the urn. I can't believe all that's left of Robert is in there. "Why didn't you want to give him a coffin?"

Robert's dad touches the urn. "I don't know. I guess it was just easier. How did you know I'd be here?"

"I heard you say something at the funeral home. And Robert always talked about the ocean. That he wanted to swim in it forever."

He smiles. "I figured this would be what he'd want. This would give him the most peace . . . the doctors say he didn't feel any pain. He died as soon as the bus hit him." Tears drop onto the urn. "He was in so much pain and felt so much guilt that he felt the need to walk in front of a bus to make things right. I dismissed his guilt over hurting Austin. I could've done so many things to help him, and I failed each time. Maybe this time I can get it right."

He opens the urn and dumps the Robert ashes into the ocean. They disappear beneath the waves. "I love you, son," he says.

He closes the empty urn and turns to me. "I'm glad somebody else was here. And thank you for being a friend to him."

"I just wish I was a better friend."

He hands me back the picture.

I shake my head and push it back to him. "I made a copy. You keep this one. When you look at it, you can see that he did get to be happy. Even if I screwed it up."

He ruffles my hair. "You're a good kid. You've had a hard week. I hope you can find peace."

"You too." I shake his hand.

I walk back to Patrick. He's trying not to cry too. He hugs me and says, "That was so brave. You did a good thing being here for him."

I cry onto his shirt. "They're both gone. Patrick, they're dead. I'm never gonna see them again. Never going to tell them how sorry I am."

He looks me in the eyes. "Yes. You will. Hopefully after a long life of doing more good, but trust and hope that you will. And until then, you don't have to go alone. You have your mom. And if you ever need to talk, or a friend, you have me too."

Patrick is a good friend. His arms aren't strong like Dad's were, but they hold me up. Maybe I will do camp again.

"Well, I'd better get you home."

I tug at him. "Can we stay just a little bit?"

He smiles and says, "You got it."

We go to a bench that looks out over the beach and ocean, and we sit until it starts to get dark. I think about Dad, Austin, and Robert. I bet Patrick is thinking about the people he misses too. We all miss so many people, but maybe we can help each other not miss them as much.

Chapter 23
Conner

"So, Austin, what do you think Santa got for you?"

"Santa's cool so I know he got me everything I asked him for. I said 'please' in my letter and left the best cookies ever and carrots for the reindeer. See? Look at all of the presents under the tree."

"Hey, short stuff, maybe all of those presents are for me."

"Yeah right, Con. At least half of those are for me."

"I thought all of them were yours. Maybe only one of them is."

"Hey boys, stop fighting. It's Christmas. No fighting allowed. Mom's rules. I'm sure Santa brought both of you more presents than you know what to do with. So why don't you both go open them? I only have so much battery life in this thing."

I press the pillow against my chest and cry into it. I was so happy that day. So was Austin. We got everything we asked for and played with the toys all day. And then Austin made us sing "Happy Birthday" to Baby Jesus.

I close my eyes as the video of us last Christmas plays. I hear the sound of wrapping paper tearing and Austin and me so surprised at all the cool things we got. I look at our red Christmas pajamas and our Santa hats. Austin's were new and every time he stands up, they start to fall down. I help him keep them on, so we don't have to see his ugly underwear.

Then we give Mom our gifts, and she is so happy. Austin got her a snow globe with Little Boy Jesus in it. She keeps it in the china closet. It was much better than my gift.

Austin kisses Mom and tells her he loves her.

We wave goodbye to the camera and say, "Merry Christmas" and promise to see the camera again next time. Then the movie stops, and the menu pops up.

"If I had known . . . I would've recorded you two a little bit longer." Mom walks in with a large photo album and sits next to me.

"He loved Christmas." I rest my head on her shoulder. "He woke me up so early. He couldn't wait to start Christmas. But I told him we had to wait for you to wake up."

"Actually," she says, pulling me closer. "I woke up before either of you. I just liked listening to you two talking."

I laugh and pull her close. "Silly Mom."

"Did you ever find out where he got the snow globe?"

I shake my head. "Nope. Lots of stores had snow globes but none like that."

"I guess that's one secret that will stay secret."

I reach for the photo album in Mom's hand and

open it.

The first picture is one of me just after I was born. I'm still all bloody, and then in the next, Dad's holding me, and I have a blue cap on my head. I skip ahead to the pictures of Mom with Austin in her belly. There's one of me touching it. She was all big and round with Austin in her. Then there's one of Austin just after he was born. He was smaller than me, but otherwise we look a lot alike then. We have pictures of all of us holding him, his first bath, his first haircut. There's pictures of us on Christmases and Easters, birthdays, and just playing. Mom has a picture of us in the tub when we were littler. You can see our parts. I hide them and say, "Mom, why?"

She laughs and says, "You're my little boys, and you two were little kids. Stop being ridiculous, Conner. Nobody else sees them."

"Moms are so weird."

She kisses my head, and we flip a page.

There are pictures of our camping trip. Austin's standing over the campfire, and there's one when he tried to catch a fish. Tried.

Then there's one of Austin just talking. It's funny because he's wearing a shirt that says he needs help because he can't stop talking.

After a few more pages, Dad isn't in the pictures anymore.

The recent pictures make my stomach hurt even more. There's some of my birthday from a month ago. There's one of Austin being goofy. There's stuff of us after a bath. At least we have towels around us in this one.

We look through the album again, and see pictures we didn't look as close at the first time. My cousin's wedding. Austin danced in front of everyone. He always made his own dances up. Us eating. Us making funny faces. Me at my Communion. Every picture is a memory. Even the ones I don't remember, I feel them.

The next page had pictures from the previous Halloween. I was dressed in a cowboy outfit, and Austin was dressed as a mini police officer.

"Those costumes were so cute." Mom touches them with a smile.

"I look stupid."

"Nonsense, you look great."

"All I know is Austin got too into it and started arresting me for not playing with him."

Mom takes out her digital camera. "I haven't gotten these printed yet, but they're from last week."

We scroll through them. Most of them are from Austin's birthday. Waking up. All the birthday stuff around the house. His party. She even got him mid-breath in blowing out the candles. Him playing with everyone. He looks so happy.

I think about my camera that Austin and I broke. I wonder what pictures were on it. I wish I could look at them, but I can't be mad at Austin. Not even a little.

Mom scrolls through more pictures of us.

The last one makes me sick. It's us sleeping that night. We're cuddled close to each other and look peaceful. Our arms are around each other.

"Mom . . . when did you?"

"I woke up in the middle of the night, and I checked on you two. It was so cute, and I had to snap a picture. I was afraid it'd wake you, but you both slept through it."

The last picture we'll ever have of Austin. I wipe my tears away. "You make sure we print a lot of copies."

Mom nods and hugs me closer.

"We gave him a good life, right?" Mom's voice is shaky.

I nod. "He was happy. He made us happy too."

We play another video on the DVD, and it starts with Austin laughing. Hearing his voice hurts, but it also helps. I hope God's letting him watch with us.

Chapter 24
Conner

I'm 11 today. It's been almost a full year since Austin died but not yet. It still hurts every day, but I can sleep in our room now. I'm doing good in school. Mom is working less, but we still have enough money to not starve.

Mom got me a small chocolate cake, and we light candles on it. She sings "Happy Birthday," and I blow them out. I make a wish I know won't come true. But it's my wish, and I'll never stop wishing it no matter what.

Mom takes me to the playground. I'm getting a little big for this. But the swings make me feel close to Austin.

As I swing, Patrick comes up to me and asks me if I can help him with something inside. Camp last summer was so much fun. I met a lot of friends, and Patrick was great. Mom was so happy that I was able to laugh again.

She sees Patrick and waves me on to follow him. I don't know why they're making me work on my birthday, but I like helping so I do it.

Patrick walks me inside and suddenly all my new

friends are there, and they shout "Surprise!" and run to me and hug me. There's food everywhere and it looks good.

I turn to Mom and she smiles. She was in on it.

Patrick pats me on the back. "You've been a great help to us all year, and now we want to do something special for you."

It is special. I feel happy again. Even though I wish Austin was here.

I'm going through the things in my room. We haven't cleaned it since Austin died. But it's time.

I put his toys from the floor in a box and stick them in our closet. I still want to keep them for now.

I dust off his parrot statue on our shelf. I want to make sure I take good care of it. It was Austin's and he loved it.

On the bottom of our shelf, I see a digital camera. It's my camera. But I thought it was broken. It was cheap and took blurry pictures. Somebody gave it to us that last Christmas with Austin. I forget if it was Santa or Grandma. But I remember one day Austin and I were wrestling and it broke. I wanted to throw it out, but Austin said he would try and fix it. Austin couldn't fix anything. But the screen isn't cracked anymore. I don't know how he did it or why he never told me. But it's fixed.

I turn it on. The battery symbol is almost empty. I'm surprised it even works.

I click on the pictures icon. And I see him. Smiling in bed. Peeking around a doorway. My pictures aren't as good as Mom's, but then I see pictures just of our feet or hair or half our face and chuckle. Those are the ones Austin took. He can't focus. But I smile at them. Even seeing his eye makes this like a buried treasure.

There's one video on it.

I never remember him taking a video. It was from my last birthday.

It's of Austin. He's trying to hold the camera to himself. The picture is shaky, but I can see his face again. His smile. I hear him laugh.

"Hey Conner! It's your birthday and that's so cool! That means you only have to play with me if you want to. But you'll want to play with me anyway. Because we're the bestest brothers in the whole world, and we love each other. Your birthday is gonna rock so much. I can't wait for you to see what we got you. And next year, I promise I'm gonna get you something really big." He stretches his arms out. "Like super huge ginormous! You won't even be able to fit it in our room, and Mommy will yell but you'll love it and that'll make me happy." He waves. "Love you, Conner. Brothers rule!" He sticks his tongue out and shows the red of his eye before the video stops.

Then the screen shuts off. The battery must really be dead now. I look in Mom's room for a charger cable. I see a dusty one under a picture of Austin as a baby. I brush off the dust and run back to our room, plugging it in underneath our lamp.

The screen comes back on, and I see his face again.

My heart hammers against me and hurts my chest. I don't cry, but I think it's because my tears are empty for a while.

Austin was right. He did get me a good gift this year. I play it again and lay down on his bed. I can't smell him anymore, and the sheets have been changed. But I still feel him when I'm in here.

Because of Austin, I was a brother. It was the best thing in the world. And even if he's not here anymore, we're still brothers, and we'll never stop being brothers.

Chapter 25
Austin

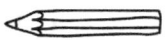

I died one year ago today on earth time. My body is all decayed now, but my soul is with Jesus and Mary and all the good people who ever lived. Like Daddy.

God lets us watch closely when somebody prays for us or visits our grave or says a Mass for us.

Conner rides up on his bike to the cemetery where they buried me. He used to come every few days but now only comes every few weeks. He might come even less soon, but that's okay.

Mommy hasn't come much. But today, she's here. She is behind Conner on her bike. I never saw Mommy ride a bike before, but she looks cool on it.

They walk up to my grave and sit down in front of it. They touch the stone they put on it that has my full name on it. "Austin Michael Palmer." It says the day I was born and the day I died, which is exactly 7 years and 3 days later in earth time.

There's no time up here. It's just always now. But we still have things that didn't happen yet like in time. Like Conner isn't here yet. He's still alive, and I think he's supposed to stay that way until he's super old. Like 92.

My stone also has a carving of Little Boy Jesus on it. It's so nice. Jesus was a little boy like me once.

They talk to me and tell me how great things are. Conner has new friends, and Mom has more money from work.

They say that Robert's dad is helping poor kids learn to read. Robert is so proud of him. I want to tell them that Robert got to go to heaven. He was sorry for what he did. In his last second alive, he wanted to not die, but it was too late. But Jesus says they'll see him when they get to heaven. That it's better they still pray for him now because there are lots of people who have nobody to pray for them, and prayers for us can still help them.

Conner looks so much bigger than before. I won't get to get bigger, but I'm not sad. Heaven is so nice and nobody has to want anything ever again, except for the people they love to come up and be happy too.

I reach out and hug Mommy and Conner. I don't think they'll ever feel me, but maybe they will feel something.

I kiss them on the cheek. They stop just a moment. Maybe they really did feel it this time.

They stay a bit, and then they get up to go because they can't stay forever. We're still a family, but we have to be apart while they are alive like they're supposed to be. God says He has a lot of good plans for them. But one day they won't have to go, and everyone will be more happy than they ever could be. We'll all be one big happy family with all of heaven forever and ever and ever. But no matter how many people we're happy with, Conner and me will always be the bestest brothers of all time.

Questions for Discussion

Teachers and parents may find it helpful to use some of these topics as opportunities to start conversations with younger readers.

1.   Austin and Conner show they are close in several ways, most notably in their ability to be open with each other. Do you have anybody that you feel you are close to in that way? What do you think shows how close you are? Are there any ways you can improve how you show this other person that you care?

2.   Have you ever had to deal with a bully? Have you ever bullied somebody else? What do you think are healthy ways to deal with a bully? What do you think a bully can do to make up for hurting others?

3.   Have you ever visited a loved one in a hospital? Have you ever been in a hospital as a patient? Did these times frighten you? What are ways you think a hospital can be made less frightening?

4.   How did you feel when Austin died? Have you ever known anybody who has died in real life? How did that make you feel? What do you think you can do to make living without this person easier? What can you do to help somebody who is grieving?

5.   Do you think if Conner knew that Austin was going to die so soon that he would have treated him differently in the days leading up to Austin's death? If you knew somebody you cared about was going to die soon, would you treat them differently?

6.   In the book, we see what happens to both Austin's body and soul after he dies. What do you believe happens when we die? What do you do when you meet people who believe differently than you?

7.   What do you think about how we treat the bodies left behind by those who have died? Do you ever think about why we use coffins and gravestones? Do you think there are things we could differently? Why or why not?

8.   Do you think Conner handled Robert's actions in the right way? If not, do you understand why he acted the way he did? If so, why do you think so? Is there anything Conner could have done differently? Is there anything those around Conner could have done differently? If you could tell Conner something right after Austin died, what would you say to him?

9.   Robert makes a drastic choice toward the end of the book to end his life. This choice brings a lot of pain to those who knew him. What do you think about this? What do you think Robert should have done differently? Do you think anybody could have seen the signs and stopped him? If you could have

found Robert before he hurt himself, what would you have said to him?

10.   Losing a loved one to suicide can hurt you for the rest of your life. What would you say to Robert's dad if you could talk to him after he lost Robert? What would you say to Conner if he blamed himself for what Robert did?

11.   How do you think you can help somebody who has lost a loved one to death to heal while still keeping the memory of their loved one alive?

12.   Do you ever think about your own death? Are you afraid to die one day? How do you want people you know to remember you after you're gone? What can you do today to start making life better for those you know?

13.   After reading this book, do you look at your own family and friends any differently? Is there anything you want to say to your parents or your siblings that maybe you didn't say before?

Things to Do

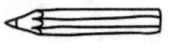

1.   Think of somebody you know that has died. Do something to honor them. Make a collage of their life, or write down things you remember about them. Maybe write them a letter.

2.   Research somebody you never met who has died. Maybe somebody who was your age when they died. Write a letter to them. Maybe write a journal entry about what you think it would have been like to know this person when they were alive.

3.   If you have siblings, write a letter to them telling them why they are important to you. Read that letter aloud to them. You may also want to try doing the same for a parent or other relative.

Acknowledgements

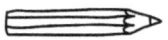

Where to begin? God has blessed me with the gift of story. Our Blessed Mother has inspired and nurtured me. My parents have encouraged and supported me. Jansina has once again been the most amazing friend/publisher/editor/formatter/ awesome person ever. She's put up with a lot more than she has to. All of my beta readers have been amazing too. Sue, Emilie, Chelise, Tammy, Lisa, and anybody who gave feedback on all or part of the book, including all of those who helped shape the story in its earlier forms (and anyone who gave feedback on the discussion questions). Emma Donoghue's Room helped shape the book into what it is now. Katy has been super amazing in capturing the pictures to use for the cover, and thanks to the boys who put up with having to model them for us. (And to their mother for allowing for the use of the pictures.) Thank you all so much. And if you played any role in the creative or production process of this book, and I neglected to mention you by name, I offer you both my thanks and apologies. Lastly, to you the reader, I offer my most sincere thanks for choosing to embark on the journey of these characters with me. I am so excited to share them with you.

More by J.J. Francesco

These books are best enjoyed by readers above age 16.

Contact the Author

www.facebook.com/jjfrancesco
www.twitter.com/jjfrancesco

Rivershore Books

www.rivershorebooks.com
blog.rivershorebooks. com
forum.rivershorebooks. com
www.facebook.com/rivershore.books
www.twitter.com/rivershorebooks
Info@rivershorebooks.com